Bob Moats

I0567277

SUNSHINE STATE MURDERS

By Bob Moats

1

Sunshine State Murders

ISBN – 978-0-9960845-9-8

For information and address:
Magic 1 Productions
P.O. Box 524, Fraser MI 48026-0524
Website: http://murdernovels.com
Cover by Bob Moats
Photo from Fotosearch.com

Bob Moats

Other Jim Richards series books by Bob Moats

For a preview or to purchase a book, go to
http://murdernovels.com

What a few people are saying about Murder Novels by Bob Moats

Mr. Moats, I just got your novel "Classmate Murders" and have to let you know, I read it in one evening. That is the first book I have ever done that with. That was the most enjoyable book I have ever read. I just started reading e-books, and reading again, after getting my wife a Kindle. This book was my 12th, and the best. I just got Las Vegas Showgirls to (read) tomorrow evening. I look forward to reading many of your books in this series. I have been searching for an author and books that were fun, entertaining reads. Your books are just the ticket.

Regards, A new fan, Bill from South Carolina

****

Another very nice comment submitted through my website from **Micki P.:**

"I recently was given a kindle for my 60th birthday. The first book I downloaded was the Classmate Murders and have now read every one of the them. Today I started on the Fatal Rejection series. Thank you for the wonderful ride with Jim and Penny and all the rest of the troop. I have laughed and giggled thru the stories, my poor family gave me the strangest looks! Now I really want a little Yorkie!! Fatal Rejection so far is another great read! I will be looking out for more of Jim Richards and since you are my #1 Author, anything of yours I can find."

Bob Moats

"I went online this morning and read your book. I thought at first that I would only read a few pages, but got sucked into it and read all 11 chapters. You are a very good writer! I read quite a bit and often pick up "Airport" paperback mysteries to read on a plane. Most of them are dreadful, with obvious plots. Classmate Murders is a much better story than most."
Ray Zink, Entrepreneur, Minn.

"I got up to chapter ten of the Classmate Murders and decided then to buy the next two books." ... "Just finished your third book, the Dominatrix Murders. I thought it was the best one of the three, didn't want to put it down till I finished it. I looked forward to see how Penny would greet (Jim) every day after her show. Keep the books coming can't wait for the next one."
Norris, Retired Naval Corpsman

Extra special thanks to:

Special thanks to Val Brooks who edited this book and for her great suggestions.

Thank you to all the people who purchased this book. I hope you enjoy it as much as I enjoyed writing it for my faithful readers.

The Jim Richards Family of Readers is listed in the back of the book.

Sunshine State Murders
By Bob Moats

Chapter 1

Earl Daws crawled across the lawn of the house looking for an opening into the place where the woman was being held. He listened for anyone speaking, to determine if it was safe to enter the building, or any movement. He heard none and so stood up at the back door to the small house, standing alone on the road at the outskirts of Las Vegas.

He looked into the back door window and saw nothing, no one moving. He carefully turned the knob on the door; it was locked. He pulled the small packet of tools from his back pocket to use to unlock the door. He worked carefully until the door lock gave way. He put his lock picks back in his pocket, pulled his Sig Sauer P250 from its holster and cautiously entered the building.

He stealthily went through the kitchen he had entered and came around the corner of an opening into the living room. He saw the missing woman tied to the chair in the middle of the room and started to go to her. He suddenly realized he wasn't alone in the room when he reached her and turned to see the shape of a man at the hallway. Earl raised his weapon and fired. The man went down just as another man came out from another room and started firing. Earl pushed the girl over to prevent her from being

6

hit, and then dove towards the second man firing his weapon. They exchanged volleys of gunfire until the man was dead. Earl stood and went to the girl, cutting her bonds and took the gag from her mouth.

"Whatcha doin' mister?" came the small voice from my right. I was startled to hear anyone so close and turned my head to see a small boy about twelve, I presumed, since I had no concept of children's ages.

"I'm writing a story," I answered the child. He was looking at the netbook I was typing on. It was a compact Acer laptop that was smaller than most laptops and only good for simple things, like writing my book stories on.

"Are you a writer?" he asked.

"I like to think I am," I replied.

"Whatcha write?"

"Crime novels," I said.

"About serial killers?"

"Well, I have written about them."

"Are you famous?"

"I'd like to think so,"

"Don't let him fool you; he's a hack writer of pulp fiction." I heard the voice from my left. It was my beautiful wife Penny Wickens-Richards, lying on the towel in the sand of the Florida beach, where we were relaxing.

"Hey, I'm a famous author," I told her then looked to the boy, "Don't listen to her, I write bestselling novels that are well read and purchased around the world.

"Are you James Patterson, I've read a couple of his books."

"No, I'm Jim Richards, author of Classmate Murders and about four other books, and I'm a well-known private eye in Las Vegas," I said.

"Never heard of you, sorry," he said then ran off when he heard some woman calling the name Henry.

Penny was laughing on her towel and I said to knock it off. "He's too young to read my books anyways," I defended.

"Oh, but he reads Patterson. Probably all his Alex Cross books with all the guns and guts and danger."

"Go back to sleep and burn in the sun," I mumbled.

She sat up and looked around the beach, now going sparse with people. "It's getting late, shall we go eat?"

"Sure, I can use a meal. We've been out here all day and didn't even have lunch. You never made it into the water."

"With all that yucky salt water, eeyu. No thanks, and I'm not fond of sharks. Sharks don't come into my living room to bother me, I'm not going into their living room to bother them."

"Well, you can swim in the pool of our motel after we eat. Shall we try some nice seafood place?"

"Sure, that sounds good; somewhere that serves lobster and shrimp."

"And some good beer," I replied.

Penny stood and nudged our toy Yorkie, Willy, who was sound asleep under my beach chair. He growled and looked up.

"Hey mutt, don't growl at me." Penny scolded. "I'll throw you in the ocean for shark bait if you do that again."

Willy stood, shook the sand off and bounced around Penny's feet.

She bent down and picked him up. "Where did your admirer go off to?"

"His mother called him," I said as I put my netbook into the case and stood. I folded the beach chair and the umbrella I sat under as Penny was picking up her towel and put it in the basket with the rest of our beach stuff.

"That's what usually happens to most of your book

fans, their mother calls them."

I stuck my tongue out at her and went off to the car sitting in the parking area, followed by my wife and dog.

We put our beach things in the car's back storage and I returned the umbrella and chair to the small rental booth, getting my deposit back. I pocketed the money and stood looking out to the water at all the boats jockeying for a good spot to anchor. We arrived in this part of Florida yesterday and I had a nice evening at a local bookstore signing my books. Today we just rested and enjoyed the beach before we went to the next stop. I heard Penny yelling about her being hungry so went back to the car, just after Penny drenched her body in the public shower to wash off the sand.

She was in and buckled safely, Willy on the seat next to her. The rental SUV was comfortable and paid for by my book publisher. They usually don't foot the bill for promotional book tour expenses now that the publishing world was hurting from all the new writers who were self-publishing their works with their electronic books, called eBooks. Even some of the seasoned bestselling authors were having their books changed to the new rage, ever since the Kindle reader came out. Sony had their own device and various other electronic book readers were now popping up for people to read the thousands of books out there.

I had my first book about the classmate murders converted to the Kindle and was available on Amazon. Sales were doing well for both the printed book and the ebook, so I was happy. So was my publisher, who agreed to foot the bill for the trip.

We were on the end of the second week of my promotion tour around the country. We left Las Vegas and all our friends and journeyed up to Reno, then over to Salt Lake City, Denver, Kansas City then to St. Louis. We even stopped for a few bookstore signings in Michigan where we were able to see our family and friends there. Even though we both were from Michigan, we considered Las Vegas as our home. I was going to sign books for a month at various big box bookstores and a few independent bookstores, hopefully to promote my new book coming out, about the Strip Club Murders. The book tour was doing well, every store had enough people to make the trip worthwhile and make my publisher happy.

We found a seafood restaurant easily enough; they were as plentiful in this area of Florida as Burger King. We went to a nice sit down meal, Willy in his travel bag watching some kids being annoying to their parents.

"I'm glad my son is all grown up and married; now he can enjoy my grandson's youth. I just don't want to have to go through it again," I said.

"Yeah, well, being senior citizens means not having children to take care of," Penny said with a smirk.

"Unfortunately, with the economy many people are moving back in with their parents and annoying the hell out of them."

"You would never do that, would you?" she said.

Sunshine State Murders

"You know I only lived with my parents to help take care of my dad." I defended.

"Sure, that was good of you, but then you moved in with me. I'm beginning to wonder about you."

I just sat staring at her as she read her menu. "I'm not some sponge, I carried my weight and did alright for myself."

"Yes Sweetie you did. Now let's get some food." She waved to the waiter and he came over to take our order.

"Where's your book signing tomorrow?" Penny asked.

"Some town called Palatka, just west of Gopher Ridge," I said with a smile.

"Why do I feel like we are in the middle of nowhere? When do we get to go to Orlando?"

"In a few days, then we return the car at the Orlando airport and fly on the corporate jet to Washington D.C. and then up to Maryland. All in due time babe."

Our food arrived and we were starving, finishing the lobster and shrimp off in record time. I sat back and took a drink of the one beer I was allowing before we drove back to the motel, where I would have a few more beers, for both Penny and me. I was watching the people in the restaurant and noticed the same kid who questioned me on the beach. He saw me and waved, I waved back. Penny caught my wave and looked back to see some gorgeous blond sitting facing me. Her head snapped back and gave me a glare.

"Hey, I was waving to the kid from the beach over just past the blonde." I defended quickly.

She looked back and saw the boy then turned and said, "Okay, but you did see the blonde."

"I couldn't help not seeing her; she's right in my line of sight to the boy."

"You better just keep her only in your line of sight buster, or you are dead," she said with a small smile.

I leaned over and said, "Murder most foul, my dear."

*

Chapter 2

We finished at the restaurant and headed back to the motel. Penny went straight to the pool and was swimming as Willy and I sat poolside. Willy looked up to me and then ran straight to the pool and jumped in. Penny was laughing at the pup, and swam around keeping an eye on him.

The motel was just about empty, only three other rooms occupied besides us. I watched as some older man in his eighties, I guessed, came out of one of the rooms and over to the pool. He stood on the edge and watched

Sunshine State Murders

Penny swimming then turned to me.

"She yours?" he asked with a nearly toothless smile.

"Yep and she carries a gun, so be careful."

"I don't see where she carries it in that sweet bikini."

"That's all right, I have mine," I said as I lifted my gaudy floral shirt showing the Glock in its holster clipped to my belt.

"Oh, I see," he said, then turned to go back to his room, just as an overweight, mean looking woman came out and yelled to him to get the hell back in the room. Poor guy, maybe I should loan him my gun.

Penny swam over to me and asked, "What was that all about?"

"An admirer, don't ask for any more," I said. She got out of the pool helping Willy onto the concrete. She came over, plopped down on my lap and licked my ear.

"Hey not fair, I'm dressed, and I'm now wet," I protested.

"Well, let's go into the room and fix that problem." She stood and took Willy back to our room. Luckily, we were about six rooms from the old man; I didn't want to give him a heart attack.

We pulled out the clean bed sheets we brought with

us and put them on the bed after I checked for bed bugs. I actually didn't like staying in motels because of the cleaning issue. I saw too many TV programs on sanitary conditions in motels and it scared me. Penny was worse than I was; she was very squeamish when it came to insects or bugs in the house or in this case, the motel. I checked the room carefully when we arrived and it looked clean, short of running a black light to see any blood or bodily fluids.

I tried to stop thinking about disgusting things and concentrated on Penny in her black teddy as she came out of the bathroom. Another breeding ground for germs, damn, was I getting so old I couldn't hold my attention on her great body.

We frolicked on the bed for a good long time. We were going for a record as to how many motels along the tour we could have sex in. This was number ten.

We cuddled after a while and fell asleep. It was a quiet night and there were no disturbances to wake us. We awoke the next morning and packed our things putting them in the car. I put the room keys on the dresser for the cleaning people to take and I left a good tip. I remembered the hotel housekeepers from our adventures in Vegas and how they helped us track down killers. I said after that I would always tip the housekeeping well.

We got into the car and drove down the 207 heading towards Palatka. I had explored Wikipedia last night and read about the colorful history of Palatka and the various takeovers by foreign countries and tribal nations. The town had about 11,000 people within the town borders and was the home to the St. Johns River State College. The town was well known for its local festivals, most notably the Florida Azalea Festival and the Blue Crab Festival.

We found a small motel on the edge of town, and went in to register. The place was half-full and we got a room away from everyone. The downside, there was no pool, Penny wasn't happy. But we would survive. I called my publisher and said we were in town, and to let me know where I was supposed to be signing my books.

He told me about the small independent bookstore on the main street and I took down the address. I finished and hung up. Penny was looking out the front window and said, "Kind of a quaint place, but I could be wrong."

I took her hand, lifted Willy and went out to the car, driving into town and found the main street area. I saw the bookstore I was to appear at later today and parked in front. We went in and there was a young girl behind the counter with a pile of my books on display. She looked to me and her eyes got large.

"Hey, you're Jim Richards! I'm so happy you are here. I'm Missy." She emoted an exuberance that bordered on scary.

"Yes I am, and this is my wife Penny Wickens-Richards."

The girl's eyes got even larger now, "Yes, you are the TV talk show woman. I used to watch you all the time before you moved to Vegas. We can't pick up your new show from there, which is a disappointment. I'd love to visit Las Vegas."

"It's a great place; you should go there at least once," Penny said and shook her hand as the woman held it out.

I asked, "Is Ken Parker here, I was told he was my contact."

"Ken is in the back, I'll call him," she said then got on an intercom and called for the man. About three minutes later he came out. He was an older man, probably in his sixties, like me. He had a good head of hair but it was a snowy white and he walked with a cane.

"Jim Richards! How great to have you here. We have a good number of crime lovers in our town and they are all waiting to meet you. Hope you are ready to sign a lot of books. I ordered two dozen more in case."

I thanked him and asked how business was. "It's been good, for an independent bookstore, we do well. Thankfully, the big stores haven't cut us out of the picture, our customers like the personal service we provide."

"I'm glad, I always like the corner bookstores. More friendly and homey," I said.

"Have you settled into a place to stay?" he asked.

"Yes, we are all checked into our motel and anxious to meet the people."

"Well, they are anxious to meet you."

Sunshine State Murders

The bell on the door rang as an older woman in her late fifties came in. She came up to the counter and looked to me. "Aren't you that murder novel writer?" she asked.

"Yes, I am, thank you."

"I hate murder novels; give me a good romance book filled with gratuitous sex and some violence, that's my cup of Joe." She said with a straight face and asked Ken, "Has my book came in yet?"

Ken came to the back of the counter and reached up to the shelves marked "Hold" and brought down a small paperback handing it to the woman. "Here it is Martha, just came in today. That will be $6.99."

"Put it on my account, Kenneth." She turned to me, "I'm not against you Mr. Richards, I just don't care for murder novels and detectives. But you have a nice day now." She turned on her heels and went out as quickly as she came in.

Penny leaned to me and said, "That was one strange woman."

Ken heard her and said, "She is part of the Bible Belt Baptists that inhabit this area. They don't like murder novels but they sure do like sex and romance books. One of the main landmarks for finding your way around here is a sleezy looking, faded red barn, it's a porn shop with peep shows and no windows. I'm from the north, New York, and I thought I got away from all the sleaze up there."

Bob Moats

I laughed and asked where we could get a good meal, he told us were to go. I said I'd be back later for the signing and we went out to our car. I stood before getting in and looked around to the brick buildings that were built years ago to replace the wood buildings that burned down in a big town fire. Penny asked what I was doing.

"I'm just studying the architecture of the street," I said as I got in the car and we drove over to the restaurant Ken recommended. We pulled up to the building and got out. The place was half full of people who all seemed happy and talkative. We sat in a booth looking out on the vehicle we rented and then a slim woman reminding me of Flo from the TV show 'Alice' came up to take our order.

"How y'all both doin' folks?" she said with a drawl that could be sliced and served on toast. "Watcha all havin' for today?"

I looked to her nametag and, honest to God, it said Flo. I stifled a laugh and said, "How are you doing today, Flo?"

"Ah'm fine, how's about you?"

Penny realized that I was trying not to laugh out loud and said, "Well, Flo, we're good and would like your breakfast special."

"You betcha, honey. Two orders of our eggs and bacon coming right up," she said and went off.

"You're going to get us in trouble yet," Penny said to me.

"I'm sorry, I suppose people from the South think we're weird too."

"No one is weirder than you my sweets," Penny said and patted my hand.

*

Chapter 3

Flo brought our breakfast to us and stood looking at me. I was concerned that she caught my finding humor in her name, but she smiled and said, "Ah know y'all. You're that writer fella, ain't ya?"

"Yes, I'm a writer; I hope I'm the writer you're thinking of," I said.

She looked to Penny and said, "Yes, you are that writer fella, and this here's y'all sweet little wife, the famous Penny Wickens. Ah'm delighted to meet y'all."

Penny smiled and said, "Thank you Flo, it's nice to be recognized. Do you read my husband's books?"

"Ah shore do, Ah'm going to y'all book signing tonight, to get ma copy signed." She said then went off to help another customer calling for her.

Penny grinned and said, "See the South does like y'all books."

"Don't you start talking like them. I'm trying to get the speech patterns out of my head from just listening to Flo," I said as I started to eat my eggs and bacon.

Willy was on the seat next to me half in his travel bag, and I slipped him a couple pieces of bacon, since they piled it on the plate pretty full. Flo came back again and spotted Willy.

"Why, what a cute puppy. Is this Willy?"

"Yes it is." Penny answered.

"Ah read about him in one of y'all books. Don't rememba which one. Ah'll go get him a plate of something he maht like." She went off and I started to laugh again to myself.

"Quit that, she's being nice."

"I know, Ah'm just enjoying this whole thing."

"You can stop with the accents, you butcher it."

"Sho nuff, honeydew."

Willy gulped up his food and we said thanks to Flo, I dropped her a five for a tip and we left to go back to the car. We drove around town and passed the red porno barn. "Want to go in and see if they have Tandy Messner's videos?" I said referring to the porn actress who was kidnapped while being bodyguarded by our friend Angelo, the mob enforcer who moved into our guesthouse. We saved her from harm and now we left Angelo in our guesthouse to watch our home while we were on the tour. I called him almost every night to see how everyone was doing back home.

"I don't really think it's good for your image to be seen going into the porn shop. I'll pass."

"Okay, but I hope the motel has an adult channel on TV."

"Why are you getting so fixated on porn now?"

"Ah'm sorry ma'am, but y'all sexy body makes me think ah nothin else."

"Will you quit that. Let's go back to the motel and get ready for your book signing."

"Yes ma'am," I said and headed back to the motel. I drove around trying to find it, but happened to come down a road and saw the sign ahead. We pulled into the lot and parked, getting out and going back to our room.

There was a note taped to the door, I pulled it and read, "Jim, I'm Val Brookside, your book editor. Your publisher told me you were in the area, so I came to meet you in person. I'm in room 34, please come down with Penny and meet me."

I showed it to Penny and told her, "Val has been

editing my books since just after the first. Morty, my publisher hooked me up with her, but I never met her. I knew she lived in Florida but not where. This is a pleasant surprise. Shall we go visit before we get ready?"

"Sounds good to me. I may need her to edit my book when I get further into it."

"You're still working on that, I thought you gave up?"

"I'm just taking a break, I'm not done yet. I need a professional to look at it and see if I'm doing a good job."

"Well, Val would be able to take on that task. Let's talk to her."

We went around the building and found the room, I knocked and after a minute, the door opened. I was surprised. The woman looked a lot like Penny, same body size, hair and facial features were the same. If I didn't know, I'd say they were separated at birth. People wouldn't mistake her for Penny, face was a bit too different, but on first look, she could pass.

"Jim, I recognize you from your book picture, and you are Penny, I've watched your show. Come in please." She stood back so we could enter.

"I understand that you live in Florida?" I said.

"Yes, about eighty miles from here, I didn't want to take a round trip drive all in one day, so I checked into this motel for the night. Morty said you were here when I called him. I'm glad to finally meet you. I enjoy editing your books."

"Well, Penny is working on a book also, an autobiography. Maybe you could edit her book also?"

She looked to Penny and said, "Sure, send me the file like Jim does and I'll take a look at it."

"Thanks, Val, I appreciate that. I'll send it when we get back to Vegas."

"Please sit and we can talk. Just let me know when you have to leave for the book signing."

We sat and then Penny asked, "How did you get into this business?"

"I had a friend who was a writer and I had taken a number of courses in literature, English, grammar and so on. My friend asked me to check his book for him and I got involved. I enjoyed working with words and my friend's publisher asked me to help them with a few of the books they were working on. The rest is history; I've been doing this for about five years."

"So Jim's books aren't the only ones you edit?"

"Oh no, I have about six I'm working on presently. Sometimes it gets blurry when I have so many books to read, they all blend together."

"Well you must enjoy it enough to put up with that," I said.

"Yes, it's a challenge sometimes though, but I get through."

We talked for about an hour and then I said that I had to get ready for the signing. "Are you going to be there? We can all go in the same car if you don't mind," I said.

"No, I don't mind, that would be nice." She gave me a business card with her cell phone number. "Just call when you are ready to go and I'll come down."

We said our good-bye for now and went back to our room. I just wanted to rest for about an hour and then get my mind into talking and signing. Penny was in the bathroom with Willy, getting her hair done up and then came out and said, "Why don't you lie down for a little while, I'll wake you in time to go."

"Thanks babe, I may do that. The signing is around six so get me up by five so I can be fresh and awake."

I went to the bed and reclined. Penny turned on the TV low and sat with Willy watching some show about Ireland on the Discovery Channel. I drifted off finally.

Around five Penny gently woke me and I sat up on the edge of the bed, shaking the cobwebs in my head. I wasn't crazy about napping, because I always had dreams that were too real and they would upset me if it was a strange story in my head. I had always been a vivid dreamer; I would create places and people that were so real I couldn't tell sometimes if I was awake or dreaming. I think it helped to write my stories though.

Sunshine State Murders

I went into the bathroom and washed up then changed into nicer clothes. Penny was still watching the Discovery Channel, now in Greece. I came up to her and gave her a big kiss, then said, "Shall we go?"

We called Val and she came around to our room, then we went to our rental car. I drove them over to the bookstore, called Books Dreams are Made Of. We arrived and there were already people starting to gather. I found Ken and he took me to a table where I was to sign from.

I was standing by the table waiting for six o'clock to arrive so I could start. The room was filling up now, I saw Flo, she waved and gave me a big smile as she held up three of my books. Penny and Val were by the counter and seated in two chairs that Ken brought out. We had introduced Val to Ken and he was happy to meet a real book editor.

I was getting ready to start when this woman or rather an older girl came up and said, "Mr. Richards, I really love your books, they are so real to me. I have read all of them at least three or four times. I almost know the words."

"Well, thank you…"

"Oh, I'm sorry, I'm Bonnie Richner and I'm from Atlanta. I missed you when you came through the one day. I was in a hospital, for a minor illness. But I found out where you were going and followed you here."

I was wondering if her illness was physical or mental,

by the way she was looking at me. I thanked her and said I had to start. Ken came forward and got the crowd settled and introduced me.

"Ladies and Gentleman, book readers, I really don't have to introduce our guest if you are a follower of his books, but I'll say his name anyway, please welcome Jim Richards."

*

Chapter 4

There was a good amount of applause and I waved to start. "Thank you Ken and I'm glad to be here. I hope I can answer any questions you may have and then I will sign your books if you have them. If not Ken has a few available to sell I'm sure." It got a laugh and then one woman in front asked how I started as a writer. I talked about how I got through the Classmate Murders and thought it would be a good book to tell people about the incident, so I sat down and started writing.

I talked for about forty minutes answering questions and then finally said I would sign books now. People lined up and I sat at the table ready with about ten pens in front of me in case one ran out, I came prepared and hopeful.

Flo came up next in line and gushed about my signing her books. She said aloud to the crowd, "Everyone, Mista Richards ate in mah diner this mornin'

27

and he'all left me a five dollar tip, Ah was impressed." She smiled at me then went off with her treasures.

I was trying not to laugh again, I looked to Penny and she was holding her finger to her lips, telling me to shut up, I did.

Bonnie Richner came up finally and was gushing again. "Mr. Richards, may I call you Jim?" she asked, I said sure. "I love your books and you are just the greatest detective in the world."

"Well that's a bit of a stretch I would say. I may be good but not great."

"Oh no, you are so great, I'm always impressed. I really have all your newspaper clippings about you on my wall and I taped anything that you interviewed on TV. I am your number one fan. Really, no one is more devoted to you than I. Really!"

"Well, thank you. I'm touched. Really." Actually I thought she was touched, but was afraid to say it. I didn't know what this girl was capable of.

"Thank you so much for the signing, I'll treasure it along with all my other treasures." She gave me a big sigh and a smile and went off. I wasn't crazy about hero worship, this was my first book stalker I figured.

Penny came over and said, "I could hear all the way over there and you should be afraid, very afraid." Then she laughed and went back to Val.

Bob Moats

I saw Bonnie walk up to Penny say something to her then walk off and out the front door. Penny looked a bit surprised and pulled Willy in his bag a little closer and then reached for her purse. I knew she was carrying her .38 Smith and Wesson in it. I hoped there wasn't any cause for concern.

I excuse myself from the signing table, went to Penny and asked, "What did that loony say to you?"

She looked up to me, and said, "Nothing I can't handle myself."

"I want to know what she said." I was insistent.

"She said it was too bad I was married to you, or she would be. Then she said to watch myself."

I turned to Ken standing at the end of the counter and asked him if he knew anyone in the local police.

He asked, "Is there a problem?"

"I'm not sure, I hope not. I'm going back to finish signing, just have someone in the police come in so I can talk to them," I said and went back to the table.

About a half hour later, there was a big cop standing talking to Ken. I saw them go over to Penny, standing next to her as she was explaining the situation. The big cop was nodding and then stood looking to me.

I had one more person to sign a book for then the

evening came to an end. I stood and put the pens in a box and went to where my people were. I came up and the big cop held out his hand to shake mine.

"Mr. Richards, ah'm Lieutenant Travis Maybell, Palatka police, my wife is a big fan of yours. She was telling me about how y'all came into her diner today and she waited on you."

"Your wife is Flo?" I said surprised.

"She is and ah'm happy with her liking crime novels. Now what is the problem here?"

"I had a very overly responsive fan who made what I consider subtle threats to my wife."

"Yes, your wife told me what this person said, I think there is a case for watching this woman, but we have to be careful. There was no overt threat; just a hint but ah can put a man on watching her, if'n we can find her."

"I just met her tonight and have no idea where she came from. Well, she did say she was from Atlanta and she just got out of a hospital, but didn't say for what. I can call a friend of mine in the FBI and see what he can find out."

"That may help, ah'm wondering if we aren't getting too worked up. Your wife said she was young, maybe she just has a crush on you and it could be nothing."

"I'm a bit suspicious when any person approaches my wife for any reason. As your wife knows from reading my books, Penny has been the target of a number of threats and they usually end up in a kidnapping or worse. We have saved her on too many occasions and I don't want to be lax in this. I don't know what this woman is capable of, but when she tells Penny to watch herself, that is a threat to me. Now we both carry weapons, and we are both registered to carry, but I'd like some support from the police on this."

"Mr. Richards, if ah let you or your wife get hurt, ah better not go home, my wife will shoot me. So ah will take care of this. Ah know of your reputation as a P.I. and ah respect your abilities, otherwise ah would ask you to back off on this, but ah think you can handle yourselves."

"Thank you Lieutenant, I'll keep you informed of any occurrences we come up against. I will try to be diplomatic before using my weapon."

"That would be real nice, and save me a ton of paperwork, thanks."

I turned to Penny and Val and said, "Shall we go find a place to have a drink and a bit of food?" They both agreed and I turned to the Lieutenant, "Can you recommend a nice place for a drink and food, maybe some nice music?"

"Well there's the Crossroad Saloon, it's a bit rough but nice, just look for the motorcycle up on the pole, out on Highway 15 by West River Road. Ah kin have one of my patrol cars to escort you out there. If y'all need a ride back to y'all motel, ah can have someone drive you and your car back."

"Well thank you Lieutenant, real nice. I'll let Flo know she has a great husband."

"She won't believe you but the thought is nice." He tipped his hat and said he'd be around.

I asked Ken if he'd like to join us and he accepted. We all went out to my rental and followed the patrol car out to the small square white building with Crossroads Saloon painted in big letters on the front. There was a motorcycle on a pole which worried me a bit, if this was a biker bar. Too bad Buck wasn't here. The patrol officer got out of his car and came in with us. He identified himself as Officer Blake Shelby.

"You don't have to follow us Officer Shelby," I said.

"Ah was told by the Lieutenant to keep an eye on you folks, so ah will. Besides, ah like to enjoy myself here. It's a favorite place of mine," he said.

"Well come on in and enjoy," I said and we entered the place.

We had a bit of food and a couple pitchers of beer and enjoyed the atmosphere of the place. Our cop sat at the bar talking to the waitresses, who I'm sure he had a personal interest in. No one bothered us when they saw us come in with our cop, so we had a nice time.

Val was loosening up and Penny was being Penny. They were having fun singing to the music and dancing in the aisles. Most of the rough looking customers were a bit afraid to approach the women, as I didn't look like I was tolerating any nonsense. Besides my Glock poked out a few times from under my jacket. It helped. About two hours of partying later, we all finally gathered outside the bar, Ken went off to his car and left and Blake, as we were calling him now, said to follow him back to the motel. We did.

Back in the motel we parked and Blake said he was to sit outside for a while until he felt it was safe. I thanked him and Val headed to her room. I was standing outside our room as I watched Willy do his thing on the lawn when I heard a scream. Penny had the door open and came out to see what it was. Officer Shelby came running over from his patrol car and we all went around the building to see where the scream came from. We arrived around the back and found Val lying on the ground, blood coming from her abdomen.

Shelby got on his radio and called for an EMT. I was holding on to Val and trying to keep pressure the wound.

*

Chapter 5

We were all standing outside the ER waiting for word on Val's condition. Officer Shelby was talking to Lieutenant Maybell who was called right after we arrived at the hospital. Penny was sitting on a couch looking upset and bookstore Ken came in after Maybell called him to ask a few questions. The two of them went off to talk in private, Maybell used his cellphone and then they came back to us. Ken went to sit on the couch next to Penny.

I wanted to get out and asked the Lieutenant if he could come with me outside. He followed me out of the ER and through the entrance doors into the black of the night. As soon as I stepped outside, I took in a lungful of air and nearly inhaled about a gallon of humidity. The air was still and dripping in the Florida humidity, I really wanted the dry heat of Vegas right about now.

"I got an APB out on the girl from your description and from Ken. She has to be in a motel around the area, since she's from out of town. We'll find her."

"Thanks Lieutenant. I've been thinking on this and I am wondering if Val was attacked because of her similarity to Penny. In the near dark the attacker may have thought it could be my wife."

"Ah was thinking that very same thing. Ah noticed the sameness of the two. It's a possiblility."

The ER lobby doors opened and Officer Shelby came out. "Lieutenant, ah take responsibility for the woman being attacked. Ah shoulda escorted her to her room. I'm regrettin' it now."

"Don't beat yourself up Blake. The threat was on Mrs. Richards not this woman, so we didn't think she would be attacked. Just keep an eyeball on Mrs. Richards now, will ya?"

"Yes sir, sorry Mr. Richards for this."

"As the Lieutenant said, don't worry about it. Help now by watching my wife."

He forced a smile and went back into the ER. I turned to Maybell, "I've never had someone so focused on me, it's a scary feeling."

"Hero worship has its price. Ah feel for all the celebrities who end up with stalkers and the police can't do much unless something like this happens."

The ER door opened again and a doctor came out and over to us. "Hey Travis, how's Flo doin'?"

"She's doin' mighty fine Doc, thank ya kindly. What's the word on the woman?"

"Well, she's stable but in a coma. We got most of the wounds sewed up and stopped the blood draining into her body, she lost a lot of it."

"Can y'all give me any preliminary opinion?"

"Well, it looks like she was hit on the back of the head with a blunt object first. From cleaning the blow area, we took a good deal of dirt from the wound. Ah'd say it was a heavy flat rock she was hit with. Then when the woman was down the assailant kept hitting her in the abdomen with some kind of knife. Can't say for sure, but ah'm thinking it was possibly a small thin hunting knife. The blow put her in the coma and the shock of the attack didn't help much either. Ah've seen a good deal of knife wounds come through these doors, ninety percent were inflicted by a woman. Men use fists or guns to do their dirty work. That's just my opinion."

"Thanks Doc. It helps, keep me informed as to her condition. Ah hope this doesn't end up as a murder case."

I spoke, "Doc, I'll take care of Val's hospital expenses and appreciate all you've done so far."

"You're welcome Mr. Richards. Ah have to say ah have perused your books, very well written. Must have been scary on a few of your cases."

"They're all are scary when you are in the middle of some killer on the verge of shooting you." I looked to the Lieutenant, he nodded knowingly.

"Well, ah have to get back to check on the woman, ah'll keep y'all both informed."

We thanked him and he went back into the building. A few seconds later, Ken came out hobbling on his cane. It was a nice looking cane, shiny black with a dragon's head on the top. It reminded me of the cane Deacon used for a while when he was shot in the hip by the Classmate killer.

"Lieutenant, if you don't need me anymore, I'd like to go home," Ken said.

"Why sure, Ken, you can go and ah thank y'all for coming out to answer my questions."

"No problem. Sorry about this Jim, it's tragic. I hope they catch the person who did this." He hobbled off and I looked back to Maybell.

"I'm wearing down too. Long day, I think I'm going back inside to get out of this humidity and rest on a nice soft couch."

"You do that; ah'll keep you informed as to our search for the girl."

I handed him my card with my cell phone number and he went off.

I came back in to find Penny dozing on the couch and Blake sitting in a chair reading a magazine. He looked up as soon as I came in and nodded. I went to another couch and laid back. Luckily the ER waiting room was vacant so it was peaceful. I must have dozed off and then I suddenly felt someone gently waking me.

"Jim, get up it's morning." It was Penny and I was shocked to see sunlight coming in the windows.

"Wow, I guess I was more tired than I thought." I sat up wiping the drool from my mouth and looked over to Blake. He was still in the chair I last saw him in. "Did you stay up all night?" I asked.

"No, someone came and took my place last night after you were asleep; Ah jest got back here a half hour ago. The Lieutenant called and said he'd be in to check on us in about an hour."

Sunshine State Murders

"Any word on the perp?"

He looked at me funny and asked, "What's a perp?"

I smiled and said, "It's a term, short for perpetrator, the person who committed the crime."

"Oh, that's a good one, I'll remember that," he said with a goofy smile.

I know this is partly country backwoods, but I would think TV would educate him as to cop terms. I stood stretching and asked Penny, "Any word about Val?"

"The doctor came out about an hour ago and said she was still in a coma. But she's stable for now, they're watching her closely. Poor woman came out to enjoy herself then this crap happens. I'd like to get hold of that little bitch myself."

"I understand your feelings but it's not proven that this Bonnie did it."

"Don't defend her, you weren't the one threatened."

"I know, I'm her hero."

"Well, stop being a hero, it's getting too dangerous."

The entrance doors from the outside of the ER opened and in walked Maybell with his wife Flo. The woman came over to me and grabbed my arm gently, "Ah'm so sarry for what happin'd. How's she doin'?"

"Well she's stable but still in a coma. Thanks for coming down."

"Travis was takin' me to work and ah said to stop in to see."

"Well thanks again."

Maybell turned to Blake and said to take Flo to the diner, he wanted to visit here a bit longer. Flo gave her regrets again and left with Blake.

"The wife was concerned. So on the way to the diner she wanted to stop and say something. She's not much on words, which ah like. So any further word from the Doc?"

Penny said, "The doctor said she's stable but still in the coma."

"Well we haven't found the girl yet, she's hidin' good."

I thought about my book tour and said to Penny, "I need to call Morty and let him know what happened." I looked to Maybell and said, "Morty is my publisher, Val was a book editor for my books and works for Morty. I should go call and tell him, excuse me." I went out to the sunshine and humidity and pulled my cell phone.

After a few rings, he came on. "Jimmy, how's the tour going, sell lots of books?"

Sunshine State Murders

"Morty got some bad news, Val Brookside came to visit and she was attacked last night, she's in a coma."

"What the hell, who did it?"

"We're not sure, but they have a suspect. They are looking for her now."

"A woman did it?"

"Again, we're not really sure but it looks that way. I have a stalker now and we think this girl did it."

"Stalker? That's not good Jim. I've had a few other authors who had stalkers, it can be dangerous. Let me know how Val is doing. Does she need any help with the hospital expenses?"

I know I said I would help with that, but why not let the corporation take care of it. "Yeah Morty, that would be good, shall I tell the hospital to contact you?"

"You bet, I'll contact accounting and set up a fund for her. She's our best book editor; I don't want to lose her."

"Morty, I'm staying here until Val is either better or… well, I don't hope that doesn't happen. So cancel my tour until this is settled."

"I understand, I'll just move everything back a week for now, how's that?"

"Good, that should work for us. I'll talk later."

"Keep me informed," he said.

I said I would and we finished the call. The sun was starting to get a little intense so I went back into the hospital to be with Penny.

*

Chapter 6

About a half hour later Officer Shelby came back. "Are you assigned to us now?" I asked.

"Yep, until further notice or the woman is caught. Ah'm going to shadow y'all to keep y'all away from the perp." He grinned as if he was proud to have used the term properly.

"Well, I feel safer already." I smiled as Blake went to sit in his chair and picked up another magazine. The patrol officer was young, probably around twenty-something and had light blond hair, cropped close. He was tall, almost six feet and thin. He was a rather handsome man and I could see that the women would like him.

Penny came over to me standing in the middle of the waiting room. "I'm hungry, and I don't want hospital food. Can we go get a bite to eat?"

I called over to Blake and said, "Can you lead us to Flo's diner, we need to get breakfast."

Sunshine State Murders

He jumped up and said he'd be happy to. We followed him out to our cars and drove the distance to the diner.

We arrived and there weren't very many people in the place, must have just missed the breakfast crowd. We sat in a booth and I insisted Blake sit with us. He was happily seated as Flo came over.

"Ya'll here for breakfast?"

"Yes, please. This number four looks good, I'll have that and Blake is eating with us, so pick something," I said to him, he grinned and asked for a number three. Penny asked for the number four also and then Flo went off.

Blake finally asked, "What's it like to be a big city private eye, especially in a city like Las Vegas? I've never been farther away than Gainesville."

"Well you have to come out sometime to visit. Being a P.I. is like any other police work, just bigger crimes in a city like Vegas. More people making it harder work to track down a serial killer or a terrorist. But we have smaller crimes also, like any other city. Have you ever had a big crime here?"

"Oh, we have our share. Lots'a poor folk here. They get a little testy when they drink and have no money to pay their bills. We don't get the serial killers or terrorist but we have our share of killings. Mostly spouses killing of spouses."

"How long have you been a cop and why?" Penny asked.

"My father was a cop here, he made Captain just after I got on the force. He was shot and killed in a shoot out with some bikers that came into town and figured they could tear up the place. The rest of our men managed to take down most the bikers. We only lost my dad." He went quiet, and I gave him the time to reflect.

"I'm sorry to hear that Blake, I'm sure your father would be proud of you." Penny offered to the man looking lost now.

He smiled at Penny's comment and said, "I'm sure he would be, my mother is certainly proud but wishes I was in some other profession."

"I'm sure," I said. "I've had many times that I wonder why I do what I do, with all the death threats and near death attempts on my life. I worry everyday about Penny, she has been kidnapped more times than any woman should be. But she has saved me a few times."

"Well Jim has this curse that murder follows him. Every time he is involved in a case someone dies," she said then suddenly realized that Val was still uncertain for her life. "I'm hoping Val isn't the one who dies. I mean I hope no one is murdered, this was supposed to be just a simple book tour."

"Yes, dear, and it will be," I said.

We talked a bit more then Flo came with our food. I

had eggs, bacon, ham and hash browns. That would tide me over for a while, the plate was full. We ate in silence then Ken came in the diner and stopped at our table.

"I was heading in to open the bookstore but saw you from the window. Nice to have a diner so close to my business," He said. "How's Val doing?"

"Same as last night, we're hoping she pulls through," I said.

"Well, please call me if she comes around," he said and asked Flo for a coffee to go. She went off to get his beverage.

"So how did you do with book sales last night?" I asked.

"We sold all but four of your books, it was a success I would say."

"Good, I'm glad someone is making money on my books."

Flo came back with the coffee and Ken handed her a dollar and thanked her. "Well, keep me informed," he said then went off and out the door.

Penny leaned to me, "I didn't want to say anything earlier but Ken was really hitting on Val last night at the bar. She was being nice but shot him down. He looked crushed."

I was munching on a piece of bacon and thought for a minute. "How crushed was he?"

"Well he sort of moped a bit then he just ignored her. But Val was so busy drinking and having a good time she didn't pay much attention to him. She could get loose after a few drinks I found out."

"I don't know much about her other than she is a very good editor. Her personal life is a mystery to me. I wonder how hurt Ken was being shot down?"

"Why? You think it may have something to do with the attempt on Val?"

"It's a thought, but I could be wrong."

"Don't start that again, I'm not getting into a discussion as to whether you are always right. You didn't win last time we went around about it."

I just smiled and finished my meal. Blake was wolfing down his grits and eggs, I didn't even want to try grits, it just sounded so disgusting. Then I thought of the TV Flo yelling to 'kiss ma grits' to people and wondered if our Flo ever yelled that.

We finished and Flo cleaned our table. I was watching people on the street all going about their business and thought about going to the bookstore again. We stood and I put another five on the table and waved to Flo behind the counter pouring coffee for a customer.

We were in the parking lot and I said to Blake, "The

bookstore is just down the street, let's take a walk to work off the food."

He smiled and followed us down the block giving us the tour guide explanation of the main street. In the couple blocks we walked I learned a lot about the area, Blake was a good tour guide. Penny was holding on to Willy in his bag as the pup's head was sticking out and looking around. I almost forgot we had him. He can be real quiet at times, I just worried we never left him somewhere.

We arrived at the bookstore and went in. Missy was at the counter and beamed when she saw us. "Good morning Mr. and Mrs. Richards. Hey Blake, good to see you too."

He went a little red and I figured he had an interest in the girl. He went to the counter as Penny and I went over to where Ken was setting up a book display. "Hello again Ken, ready for the new day?"

"Sure am Jim. I received a new shipment of books, I always like when they come in. It's like Christmas Day for me opening the boxes. All the bright shiny books packed inside. It's a good feeling."

I picked up a new Robert B. Parker book, "Blue-eyed Devil" published after his death a few years back. I wish I could have met Parker, his Spenser books inspired me to become a P.I. and I enjoyed reading all the books I purchased when I was finally taking in money for my own books.

"Ken, I don't have this book in my Parker collection,

46

Bob Moats

I've never been into westerns very much but Parker makes it interesting. I'll take it please."

"For you, no charge. I made enough off you last night."

"Well thank you Ken, appreciate that."

"Are you still going on with your book tour now?"

"No, I called my publisher and we are pushing the tour back a week, hopefully Val will come around by then. I plan on taking care of her until she's well enough."

"That's mighty nice of you."

"You said you were from New York, why'd you leave to come down here?"

"I got tired of the big city and my bookstore there was being forced out by the big box bookstores. Hell, Barnes and Noble put up one of their super stores about four blocks from my store. It was just too hard to compete."

"I can understand that. How did you find this place, Palatka I mean."

"My wife and I used to come down through here on our way to Marineland on the coast. We stopped a couple times and really liked it."

"Where's your wife?"

"She passed away a couple years ago, just after we moved here. She at least got to enjoy it for a while. She had heart failure, it took her quick, thankfully."

"I'm sorry to hear that. So you've been alone for a few years then?"

"Yep, I couldn't find another woman to compare to my wife."

I looked to Penny who had an expression on her face that made me wonder. I'd ask her about it later.

"No one woman in town could peak your interest? There must have been one or two?"

He paused and smiled, "Yes, there was one woman, a school teacher last year that I was interested in but she disappeared one day. They couldn't figure what happened to her, she just vanished and they never found her. Shame, she was someone I could have been interested in for more than just an acquaintance."

I was now wondering how he considered a woman as more than an acquaintance.

*

Chapter 7

We were out on the street again and I was feeling bad for thinking those thoughts about Ken possibly hurting anyone.

Penny was quiet and I asked how she felt about our visit with Ken. "Well I just got a chill when he was talking about other women after his wife passed. I thought he was a little aggressive with Val last night. And when he said that teacher who he had an interest in disappeared. I had to wonder."

"Yeah, I had those thoughts also. Ken has been such a nice person."

"So was Jeffery Dahmer, or so people who knew him said. I understand your concern but we have no proof that Bonnie did this. It could be anyone, even an attempted robbery gone wrong on a woman alone in the dark."

"I hear you. But for now Bonnie is the number one suspect. So why is she hiding?"

"Maybe she's just sightseeing and not hiding. Maybe she doesn't even know she's being looked for."

Blake was still following and spoke, "Hope y'all don't mind if I say somthin'?"

I stopped, causing Penny to shift gears and came to a halt, Willy nearly slid out of his pouch.

"I'm sorry Blake, I forgot you were back there. What do you think?"

"Well, I've known Ken for a good number of years now and back when Dorothy, the teacher, disappeared, we did look at Ken with suspicion. But he had an excuse for the night of her disappearance."

"He had an alibi?"

"Yeah, that's the word, alibi. He had an alibi for that night. So we didn't figure he had anything to do with it."

"Well that clears that up." I looked to Penny, "So we can rule Ken out." I said that but I thought about calling Harold Kettering, my FBI friend and seeing if he could come up with anything on Ken Parker when he was back in New York.

We continued to our cars still in the parking lot next to the diner and Blake led us back to the hospital. We went in and I went to the nurse's station and asked the nurse who helped us if there was any word on Val.

"No Mr. Richards, she is still in intensive care and being watched." I thanked her and we went back out to the waiting room.

"I have the feeling we are going to be waiting for a long time; we need to go do something to get our minds off this for now. Blake, I think I'd like to go back to our motel to get cleaned up and changed." I looked down to my pants and they still had blood on them from Val. I forgot about that fact earlier when we went downtown. I hope no one saw me in this condition.

"Sure Mr. Richards, just follow me and I'll get you there." I told them I was going to give the nurse my cell phone number if anything changes. I went back to the nurse's station and gave her my card.

We went to our cars again and followed Blake to our motel. Penny and I went in and Blake said he was going to rest in his car. He was parked right in front of our room so I wouldn't worry about being attacked.

I went to the bed and plopped down on it. It was too early to take my daily nap. I hated getting older. Penny said she was taking Willy out for a walk on the lawn to do his business. I said to have Blake keep an eye on her, at least until they found Bonnie.

She went off just as my cell phone buzzed; I sat up. "Hello?"

"Jim, this is Travis Maybell, just wanted to call and tell you ah got the forensic people from Gainesville to come down and process the crime scene this morning. They found a rock with a little blood on it, three guesses whose blood it is. The doc from the hospital made a formal statement and said the wounds were from a thin blade like a stiletto, although ah haven't seen a stiletto in years. Most killers prefer hunting knives or big honking switchblades. Guess when we find Richner, we'll know. She's still hiding out, ah'll let you know if anything crops up."

I thanked him and disconnected. I stood and went to

the door and looked out. Penny and Blake were following Willy around the lawn as the pup was sniffing up a storm. Too bad he wasn't a bloodhound, I'd have him track down Bonnie. In Las Vegas, they had tracking dogs that they used often, I wondered if they had them here. Probably some backwoods trapper with a couple old coon hounds.

I hadn't talked to Buck or Trapper in a while so went back to the bed, sat and called the office. Lacey answered.

"Office of Carson, Trapper and Daws, private investigators. How may I help you?"

"You could put my name back on the title. Of course, you knew it was me. How's things back there?"

"Well, we have been busy since you left. Lots of customers all wanting their crimes solved, at least enough to pay the bills. Angelo is on a protection job for some movie biggie and is complaining about the bitching the star is doing about everything. Earl and Trapper are both out on cases, Buck is sleeping from having to cover for sick guards. Other than that all is peaceful in the office, and I'm not being frightened by you popping up."

"So all is normal?"

"Yep, all is good. Deacon and Lynn came in yesterday while they were cruising by and asked how you were doing. I told them you forgot about us, since you don't call very often. So what is going on with you and Penny?"

"Plenty of sun, lots of book sales and an attempted

murder of my book editor."

"Why, did you attempt to kill her?"

"No, I didn't. We think I have a stalker and she attacked the woman thinking she was Penny, that's what we theorize for now."

"So are you continuing on your tour?"

"It's been put on hold for now until we catch the person. When Earl gets back in the office have him call me. I may need his contacts to find out a couple things for me."

"Will do boss. Anything else you need, I'm busy here."

"Just tell everyone we are fine and miss them. Keep the home fires burning and have Earl call."

She said she would and we finished. I looked around the room thinking that it would be hard to live in motels traveling the road like singers do. I thought of getting one of those big busses and live in that on my next book tour. Would be a lot better than motels.

Penny came back in a few minutes later and let Willy off his leash. "Shall we take a shower?"

"You mean the two of us?"

"Is that so hard to imagine, we've done it enough

times before, or are you being difficult?"

"I'm never difficult, race you?"

She pushed me and ran into the bathroom. I followed dropping my clothes.

An hour later, we came out and toweled off. My cell phone had a message on it, I checked the voice mail and it was Earl.

I called him back and he sounded happy to hear from me. "Hey guy, Lacey says you are embroiled in murder? I told you that you had the death eye," he said with a hearty laugh.

"There was no death, hopefully not yet, and quit with the death eye thing. The woman is in a coma for now, but we're hoping she pulls through. I need to see if you can pull a few favors in for me."

"Shoot, I'm prime to bug a few contacts, it's been a while."

"Okay, I need some info on a man named Ken or Kenneth Parker. He had a bookshop in New York and I'm suspecting he may have some shady past."

"Shady pasts are my specialty. Anything else you may have on him to go on?"

He had a wife that died a few years ago, that's all I got. I didn't want to push the issue with the locals, he's well liked. I'm doing this on my own. Hold on." I had a thought and went to the door, calling Blake from his car. "Hang on Earl."

Shelby came over and asked what I needed. "Can you tell me what Ken Parker's wife's name was?"

"Sure, it was Linda. Why?"

"Tell you in a minute. Did he ever say what the name of his bookstore in New York was?"

"Sure, the same as here."

"Thanks Blake I'll talk to you in a minute," I said, turned into the room and back to the phone. I gave Earl the extra information.

"Well, it's not much to go on but I'll do what I can. Otherwise, how's the tour doing?"

"It's on hold for now. Please see what you can find for me."

"Will do, I'll call Harold and see if he can help also." I was hoping he'd call Harold.

"Thanks and talk later." I hung up and went back to the door and explained to Blake what I was doing.

"You're investigating Ken?"

"Blake, when it comes to crime we look into all the

people around the incident. Even nice people, they could be hiding something. Just keep this between us, I don't need people giving me a hard time."

"Your secret's safe with me. Ah like Ken but ah always thought he was a bit off," he smiled and went back to his car.

I turned back to see Penny standing, holding Willy, when my cell phone buzzed again. I answered and heard a tiny voice.

"Mr. Richards, help me."

*

Chapter 8

"Bonnie, is that you?"

"Mr. Richards, I'm scared. I think I'm going to be killed, can you help me?"

"How do you know you are going to be killed?"

"I just know, I'm in danger, you have to help."

"Where are you Bonnie?"

"I'm hiding right now, I can't say, they may have the phone bugged."

"Bonnie, no one can bug my cell phone. How did you get my phone number?"

"I called your office and said I was part of your tour and needed to reach you, some guy gave it to me."

I had to talk to someone about giving out my number. "Bonnie calm down, you're not helping me, where are you?"

"I'm running for now. I'll call back later as soon as I get to a safe place." She hung up.

"Damn, she was almost hyper." I turned to Penny still standing with Willy. "Bonnie was saying someone wanted to kill her, who?"

"Well, I don't know. Maybe she's trying to confuse the issue, pretending to be innocent."

"True, but she sounded really frightened. I have to call Maybell." I pulled my phone again and dialed his number from my caller ID recall.

He came on after a few rings. "Jim what do ya have?"

"Got a development, I need to see you; can you come to my motel room?"

"Shore, ah'll be there soon," he said and hung up.

Sunshine State Murders

I turned to Penny and checked my caller ID, the last call in came up unknown. "Maybe a disposable phone, or a payphone. Why didn't she tell me where she was, if she trusts me so much? I'm wondering."

"Frightened people do stupid things, what all did she say?" I told her. "Well, if she's on the run she can't tell you where she is."

"Yeah, I hope she lands somewhere soon. I'm worrying now. The girl may be crazy but she's not sounding like a killer. Just my opinion."

"And you are never wrong," Penny said with a smile.

"Don't start that now." There was a knock on the door and I went to open it. Blake was standing at the door and said, "Maybell called and wants me to be by you, in your room. You don't mind?"

"No Blake, it's all right. Come on in." Penny went back to the bathroom to get her clothes and came back out after she was dressed.

I had dressed too, I didn't care if Blake was in the room, I had nothing to hide other than a beer belly. About ten more minutes there was a knock on the door and Blake held up his hand saying he'd get it. He called through the door asking who it was. I could hear Maybell yell to open the door. Blake did.

Maybell came into the room and said, "What's so urgent?"

"I had a call from Bonnie Richner."

His eyes opened a bit more then asked, "And?"

"She was scared, saying someone was trying to kill her. I couldn't find out where she was, she said she had to find a place to hide and then she'd call me back.

"Now who'all would want ta kill her? She knows no one in the area."

"I don't know who she knows, but I guess I'll find out when she calls back. Now why would someone want to murder her?"

"She's an annoying stalker," Penny offered.

"I don't think that's it," I replied.

"Well, at least she's reached out. If'n when she calls, tell her we'll protect her. Tell her to let us get to her. Then we'll find out."

"Thanks Lieutenant, I'll let you know as soon as she calls."

"Ya know, y'all could have tole me this over the phone."

"But I wanted to see your smiling face," I said as I gave him a big smile.

Sunshine State Murders

"Don't fuck with me, ah don't have a very nice smile," he said then gave me a big smile and went out of the room.

I looked to Blake and he was trying to hold in a laugh, I didn't hold it in. Penny told us both to grow up and went out the door to get some fresh air she said, followed by Blake.

I put on my shoes and gathered my pocket stuff, wallet, keys, money, flashdrive and Swiss army knife. Now I was prepared. I had my cell phone in my shirt pocket where it always resided. It annoyed me when people had cell phones but you couldn't reach them because they would put it down somewhere and walk away from it. Why have a cell phone if you don't want to be called?

Penny came back in and said, "It's getting too humid out there, I don't see how these people live in this."

"We'all git used to it ma'am," said Blake.

"Well, y'all can keep it," Penny mimicked.

"We could move to a motel with a pool," I said.

"Good, I'm packing." She went over to her luggage and started to pack. I was laughing to myself and looked to Blake. "Know a motel with a big pool?"

"Ah shore do, ma cuz'in has one not far from here. I'll call and git ya a good room."

I thanked him and went to pack. I stopped and wondered about Val's belongings. I asked Blake to get her room key and asked Penny if she could also go pack Val's stuff, since I didn't want to go through her personal things. Penny said that was good and finished up packing her things and when Blake came back with the key, I asked him to follow Penny to the room and watch her. They went off and I put our luggage in the car. It was a good change of pace for us, getting away from the scene of the crime.

I called Maybell and told him we were moving, he thought that was a good idea, to confuse our attacker. He asked if Bonnie called yet, I told him she hadn't then we finished. A few minutes later Blake came back struggling with four suit cases of Val's. Penny following him with a small make-up case.

"For a woman who lived only eighty miles away, she sure packed for a long trip," Penny said as she put the suitcases in our SUV.

"Maybe she had other plans?" I said.

"Well, there was enough clothes in her room to fill a big closet. I'm wondering if she was hiding out."

"Interesting, maybe her attacker was someone from where she lived," I said. "She was on the run from this person. I'll have to check it out."

"Well, check it later; I want to get into a wet pool and out of this wet atmosphere. Don't ever suggest we move here." She finished putting her luggage in the vehicle and I checked the room to be sure we hadn't forgotten anything, like Willy. He was safely in the front seat next to Penny. I returned the room keys, thanked the manager at the office and returned to the car.

Blake said to follow him to the motel and we did. It was a nicer place, more of a southern style, lots of hanging moss and ivy, Spanish style architecture. I was sure it was made that way for the tourists, but it worked for me. We pulled in and Penny saw the pool and pronounced that it was good. We parked and Blake led us into the lobby of the office.

"Hey Blake, ya'll made it," said the older man behind the counter.

"Shore did Virgil, these are ma friends, Mr. Jim Richards and his wife Penny. Ah'm protecting them from harm. They need your best room, they's celebrities from out Las Vegas way."

"Well, any friend of Blake is welcome. I got the best room ready for y'all, and close to the pool as Blake specified."

Penny thanked him for that as I signed the register.

He gave me the keys and then we drove down to the parking space in front of the room. Blake helped us unpack the car. We put Val's luggage in one corner of the room and Penny dug out her swim wear and proceed to the pool. I swear she was born under the sign of tadpoles; she loved the water. Blake and I sat by the pool watching

Penny and Willy swim around. I was getting used to the humidity, Michigan could be a lot like this at times in the summer.

We relaxed for about an hour and then my cell phone buzzed, I answered. It was the hospital.

"Mr. Richards, you asked to be called if there was a change, Miss Brookside is drifting in and out, but she's coming around."

"Is she talking yet?"

"No, the damage to her head caused a concussion and her speech is impaired, but she's lucid."

"Thank you, I'll call Lieutenant Maybell and tell him." I hung up and called Maybell. He came on and I relayed the message. I said we would meet him at the hospital.

Penny was enjoying herself in the pool so I called her over and told her what the hospital said.

"Listen, there's nothing you can do so just stay here with Blake watching and I'll go to the hospital and see what's going on. I'll fill you in later."

"I hope she comes around, be careful." I leaned down and kissed her. I told Blake what was happening and to stay with Penny. He said he would and I went to the car and over to the hospital with Blake's directions.

I arrived and went in to find Maybell already there. He turned to me and said, "She's awake barely, but your friend can't talk, Doc says her speech is gone."

*

Chapter 9

"Permanently?" I asked.

"Well, Doc says she may git her voice back, time will tell. Shall we go see her?" Maybell said and we went to the ICU ward and found the doctor standing by Val's bed. She was looking groggy and her eyes weren't quite open, but I could see recognition in them when I came into view.

She was just lying there, not moving. I took her hand and I could feel a slight squeeze. I leaned over and looked into her face and her eyes were moving back and forth. I wondered if she was looking around the room or having a reaction to waking.

"She's still not fully awake but she started to move about an hour ago and we've been watching her. Her vocal abilities may not work due to the concussion pressure that affected the speech area of the brain. We'll be giving her an MRI when we feel she is well enough. We're watching her vitals and hope she comes out of it soon."

I thanked the doctor and then said to her, "Hey Val,

it's Jim Richards, can you hear me?" I waited for a sign, I thought I felt her hand squeeze a bit but it could be just an involuntary movement. "Val if you can hear me, give my hand a good squeeze." I waited, nothing.

I looked to Maybell and said, "She's not ready to give us anything. I'll sit with her until something happens."

"That's mighty good, let me know if'n she comes around better. I need to git back to ma duties in town. Crime doesn't wait." He said good-bye to the doctor and left, followed by the doctor.

I pulled over a chair and sat next to her bedside. I took her hand again with both of mine and hoped to feel something.

My cellphone buzzed and I pulled it out, it was Penny. I explained Val's condition and told her I would call if she comes around. I told her to ask Blake to give her a ride here if she wanted to come in and sit with us. She said she would.

I sat back watching Val as she struggled to gain alertness, trying to wake more. I could see the struggle in her still half-closed eyes.

About a half hour later, Penny came in. "Where's Willy?" I asked.

"They wouldn't let me bring him in ICU, so I had Blake watch him. He's in the waiting room. How is she doing?"

"The same, she's more awake, but still not enough to tell us anything." I stood, "Here, you can sit with her, I need the restroom." She sat and took Val's hand and I went out of the ICU finding Blake in the waiting room. He looked so funny holding the tiny fur ball as Willy snoozed on his arm.

I waved to him and went to the restroom. There was a man in there washing his hands. He looked to me through the mirror, gave a slight nod and then I went into a stall. I closed and locked the door as I heard the hand dryer blowing. I heard the restroom door open and close and I was alone. I did my business and then went out to wash my hands. As I was standing at the hand dryer, my cell phone buzzed. I shook off my still wet hands and pull the phone, it said unknown.

I answered, "Hello?"

"Mr. Richards, I'm still scared that he will kill me," came the voice of Bonnie Richner.

"Bonnie, you're sounding confused, take a breath and tell me where you are."

"I'm in a shelter for homeless. I found it after I last talked to you. Please protect me, he'll kill me."

"Bonnie, I can't help you if you don't start telling me where you are, what shelter."

"Damn, I have to go they are coming around," she said then hung up.

"Crap," I said and called Maybell.

He came on and said, "The lady talking yet?"

"No, but I just got another call from Bonnie. She said she is in a homeless shelter. You know any?"

"Shore, thars about three of them, run by the Baptists. She didn't say which one?"

"No, but if you get officers to all of them maybe they can find her."

"Gee, now why didn't ah think of that?" he said with a slight chuckle in his voice. "Ah'll send my boys out to look fer her and call y'all back." He hung up and I finished drying my hands and the now wet phone.

I went back to Blake and Willy and told him about the call. I sat and petted Willy still resting in Blake's arm. "What do ya think the woman is up to?"

I thought about it, "I'm not sure, I'm hearing fright in her voice, but she could be a good actress. If they can find her in one of the shelters, maybe we'll find out what she's up to."

We sat watching the TV in the waiting room. There was a show with doctors talking about women's problems, not something I needed to watch. I stood and said I was going back to Val. As I was passing the TV, I switched channels and found an old western movie. Blake said that would be good.

I went back to the ICU and passed the same man I saw in the restroom. He avoided looking to me and went on his way out of the ICU. I wondered who he was, he wasn't hospital staff, he wasn't dressed for it and didn't have an ID tag. I got back to where Penny was still sitting and she turned to me.

"Just had a strange thing happen, some man came around the curtain and stopped when he saw me. He turned back out quickly and went off. I could feel Val's hand really tighten on mine and she was shaking a bit."

I turned back to the doors of the ICU running now, looking for the man. I couldn't see him and went to the lobby, but he was gone. I came back to Blake and told him what Penny said, he stood and I took Willy and told Blake to go watch the women. He went off and I went outside to see if I could find the man. I went over and put Willy in the car, rolling down the window a bit then locked the doors.

I went back in to the nurse's station and found our friendly nurse. "I need to ask a question? Have there been any phone calls about my friend in the last day?"

"Why yes, some man called saying he was a family friend, asking how she was doing. Was that alright?"

"I'm sure it was but if you get anymore calls let me know right away, please."

"I will," she said. I thanked her and went to the ICU.

Blake stood from his chair with his hand on his weapon as I came around the curtain; he looked worried. "I couldn't find him, but we will have to be on alert now. I'm thinking this is something to be concerned about. Bonnie said some man was wanting to kill her and now this stranger comes around here where Val is. I'll call Maybell, I think he may get tired of hearing from me." I smiled and went out to the lobby.

I called him again, he came on sounding impatient. "What now Richards?" I thought back on Trapper's responses to my annoying calls and almost laughed.

I told him of what had happened and my suspicions. "I'm wondering if the attack was from someone who knew Val and he's making sure she doesn't talk because he didn't succeed in killing her the first time."

"Sounds valid ta me, we haven't found the girl yet, ah got all my men on the search. If'n she's in one of the shelters, we'll find her."

"I have Blake sitting with the women. I think I'm going to keep the two of them together for now."

"Ah jest hope Blake doesn't shoot some doctor, the boy gits a touch nervous. Ah'll send another officer to help. This is gittin deep."

"I agree; I'm calling a friend to see if he can find out anything about Val back in her town. Maybe she has family that can help."

"Sounds good, let me know." He hung up.

Sunshine State Murders

I dialed Earl and he came on. "Jim, I don't have anything for you yet, Harold is working on it."

"I called because our case is getting complicated." I explained to him everything that happened in the last two days.

"You want me to get some dirt on the book editor?"

"If you could, I need to know if she has an angry ex who may have followed her here. See what you can find. I'll give you the number of my publisher, he has more info on where she lives." I pulled my Palm TX, pulled up the address book and gave him the number. He said he'd get back to me with the info.

I sat down on the lobby chair and thought. What was the reason for Val's attack? On one hand we had a jealous Bonnie, then we had Ken shot down by Val, was he mad enough to attack her. Now we had an anonymous stranger who showed an interest in her. Any more killers?

I looked out the front window of the hospital now becoming busy with people, and felt tired. It was time for my nap and I wasn't ready for it.

*

Chapter 10

I was sitting in the chair when I felt someone shaking my shoulder. I opened my eyes, I must have dozed off, and saw Blake bending over me. I blinked a few times and asked, "Where are the women?"

"Officer Schmitt came and relieved me for now. Ah'm going home to get some sleep."

I looked out to the front window and it was starting to get dark. I wondered how long I had dozed. I knew we had a long day, and we needed rest. I stood and told Blake to have a nice sleep and he said he'd see us in the morning. He went off and I went back to ICU.

I came around the curtain and the officer put a hand out to me, Penny said it was alright. "He's my husband."

"Okay, Mr. Richards, good to meet you. I've heard a lot about you from the Lieutenant."

"Good or bad?"

"Both," he said with a laugh.

"You have been talking to Maybell then. Are you going to stay here for the night with the woman?"

"That's the plan. I was told about the possible attempts, no one will get past me."

"Good, I'll sleep better." I turned to Penny, "It's getting late and this has been a busy day, shall we go get some sleep also?"

She looked to Val, sleeping again and said, "I think I need it, she'll be alright for now." She stood and came to me. I handed officer Schmitt my business card, "If anything at all happens call me, anytime."

He said he would and we left. I had paid more attention to the directions to the motel from earlier and we found ourselves back and in our room. Penny didn't feel like swimming, she was thinking about Val. We just went to bed and snuggled. I was asleep quickly.

The next morning came quickly also, no one had disturbed our sleep, which was good. That meant nothing bad or good had happened during the night. I used the bathroom after Penny and then dressed. We went out of the room and there was a small restaurant across the street so we went over for breakfast. Willy was looking at my food so I gave him some of it and he rested on the bench happily wolfing down the ham slice. We paid our bill and went back across the street to the car just as my phone buzzed.

"Hello?" I answered. It was Bonnie.

"Mr. Richards I think the police are after me. I left the shelter when I saw them come in."

"Bonnie the police are trying to help you, why are you still running?" I was almost yelling now from frustration.

"They aren't going to hurt me are they?" she said nearly sounding like she was crying.

"Bonnie, stop this! Where are you so I can come to get you, now tell me!"

She was quiet for too long, "Bonnie talk to me, where are you?"

"I'm in Wal-Marts, in the cafeteria. Can you help please? No police please."

"Okay, Penny and I will come to get you; stay there and don't move, you hear me!"

"I will, please hurry." She hung up.

"Damn," I said and told Penny.

"Are you going to call Maybell?"

"No, if Bonnie even sees a cop she'll run again. I need to get there before she splits. I have no idea where Wal-Marts is." I pulled my Palm TX and hooked up with some local Wi-Fi to the Google maps and did a search. I found the place and followed the map as we drove to the superstore on Route 19 below Crill Avenue, AKA Route 20.

I drove as quickly as I could without breaking any speed limits. It was pissing me off that people were going so slow, didn't anyone have any place to go to faster?

Sunshine State Murders

We finally could see the big blue and white Wal-Mart sign coming up and pulled into the parking lot, finding a lucky space up front. We jumped out and went into the building. Penny had Willy in his travel bag and was holding him close. I asked the greeter where the cafeteria was, he pointed it out to us.

I was ahead of Penny, I didn't want Bonnie getting away before we both got there. I stood at the edge of the food tables and looked around, I didn't see her. Penny came up and I turned to her and said, "Looks like she fled again."

Penny poked my arm and pointed to the restroom doors just past the service counter, Bonnie was on the payphone next to the restrooms. I ran to her before she saw me and grabbed her arm. She screamed and turned her head to me, looking totally frightened. People were staring now and some big hillbilly looking man nearby yelled to ask if she needed help. Bonnie saw it was me and told the man no. She turned and grabbed on to me hugging tightly.

Penny came up and could see Bonnie was in tears. I pushed her back so I could talk and asked if she was alright.

"I am now, I've been so frightened. I think he's been following me."

"Okay, let's sit and talk." I pulled her to a table and we sat. She was looking like a wreck and I gave Penny some money to go get us something to drink. She went off and I said, "Just take a few minutes to calm down and wait for Penny to bring our drinks." She agreed.

I looked over to see the hillbilly still staring at me, I just stared back and pulled my jacket back exposing my Glock. I could see his eyes go to the gun and he turned his attention back to his meal. I smiled and looked back to Bonnie. I could see a couple of days of wear on her. Penny came back with a tray of drinks and some fries. She offered Bonnie the fries and the girl grabbed on and ate them like she hadn't eaten in days.

Penny sat and said, "I figured she could use some food." I smiled at my beautiful and thoughtful wife. Bonnie grabbed at the Pepsi on the tray and washed down the fries.

"I sorry for bringing you into this, but I didn't know anyone around here to go to. I don't trust police, I've had bad experiences with them in the past. I'm sorry for lying to your man in Vegas, but I needed your number to call you."

"It's alright, we're here now. You have to tell us why you think someone is wanting to kill you?" I didn't want to mention that the police were looking for her as a suspect in the attack on Val.

"I saw your friend get murdered and he saw me. Now he wants to kill me."

"Bonnie, our friend wasn't murdered, she's still alive but in critical condition. Why didn't you call the police when you saw it happen?"

Sunshine State Murders

"I called you. I knew you would help me. I was going back to my motel and I saw some man in the parking lot coming towards me. I ran and been running since."

"Okay Bonnie tell me all you saw of the attack on our friend. All the details, please."

She took another swig of Pepsi, she was out, so I pushed my cup to her and she took it. "I left the bookstore after your signing." She paused and looked to Penny, "I'm sorry if I was rude to you with what I said. It wasn't nice of me."

Penny smiled and said to forget about it.

"Go ahead with your story Bonnie," I said gently.

"I knew where you were staying, I had talked to your publishing company and they told me."

Great, now everyone is giving out my information I thought. I need to talk to a few people about privacy.

She continued, "I was standing outside of your motel waiting for you to come back. I wanted to talk to you about your books. I saw you pull up and then I saw a woman go around the building, at first I thought it was Penny, they look so much alike. I realized it wasn't when I saw Penny get out of the car and go to your room. I waited for a while to see if you'd come back out so I could talk to you, but I heard noises coming from the back of the building,

I went there and saw a man kneeling next to someone on the ground. I went over and saw it was your friend and she had blood on her. I screamed and the man jumped up and came at me, I was scared but couldn't move, then he grabbed my arm and I pulled away and ran. I should have ran to you, but he was cutting me off. All I could do was keep running and I didn't stop for what seemed like an hour. I finally didn't see him behind me, but I kept going and hid out in a culvert pipe off some drainage ditch until morning."

She stopped and took another swig of Pepsi then paused. She looked like her attention was somewhere else. I figured she was playing the incident back through her head. I waited for her to gather her thoughts and then she continued.

"I went back to my motel and realized I had lost my purse somewhere along the way. It had my room key in it and the name of the motel. That's when I saw the man in the parking lot coming towards me and I ran again. You have to help me, he knows me now"

*

Chapter 11

"Bonnie, I've made some friends in the local police and they'll want to help you as long as I explain what happened, according to your story. The police do want to question you about the attack, they suspect you did it and it didn't look good for you to be hiding. I'll talk to the cop in charge of the attack and we'll get it ironed out. Okay? Can you trust me?"

"I can trust you; you have solved many great cases. I know you will protect me from the man and from the police."

"Alright, you said you saw the man coming towards you in the parking lot of your motel. What did he look like?"

"I didn't see him very well, but he was tall, about your height, dark hair, clean shaven and he was wearing sunglasses, large ones that hid most of his face. That's all I can tell you."

"What kind of clothes?"

"Oh, I think a dark shirt and he was wearing Khaki colored pants, I remember that because they looked like police pants."

I thought about the man in the hospital and I do remember he had tan colored pants. "Okay I think we need to go talk to Detective Lieutenant Maybell, he's my contact in the Palatka police. He's a good person, and you can trust him. But first I think we need to get you cleaned up, you've been running around for a couple days and I think the sewer pipe you hid in is following you." Penny agreed and we left Wal-Marts and drove towards our motel.

"I really need to get into my motel for my own clothes, can we go there instead of your motel?"

I looked to Penny and she nodded. "Okay, we'll need to get you another key." She gave me shaky directions to the motel but we found it finally. We took her into the office and she told them she lost her key, they gave her another. We followed her to her room, I asked her if she had a car.

She gave me a shocked look and said, "It's still in your motel parking lot, the keys were in my purse but I have a spare set of keys in my suitcase. I learned to always have a spare. Can we get the car?"

"We can get it later. After we take care of talking to the police." We went into her room, it was tidy and small. She went to her suitcase and took out some clothes and then went into the bathroom. Penny was looking around the room, saw my books on the desk and pointed to them for me to see. I could hear the shower running and then about twenty minutes later she came out dressed and clean.

"Okay, now we can face the world with a better look, I'm calling my friend in the police."

I pulled my cell phone and dialed Maybell. He came on and I told him about finding Bonnie and that we needed to bring her in to explain what she told us. I didn't go into detail about it, just that we'd be in shortly. He said he'd watch for us, and threw in not to get murdered. I laughed and said I'd be careful then hung up.

"Okay he's waiting for us, let go get this taken care of." I stood, asked Bonnie for her spare keys to her car.

She got them out of her suitcase and then gave them to me. I left the room and then the women followed. We went to our rental car and I drove over to the police headquarters on the corner of St. Johns and 11th Street. It was a small tan and red building attached to huge fire department bays. We drove past it and into the parking off 11th and went in to the desk of an officer who gave us a strange stare. Did we look funny?

"Kin ah help y'all?" he said with a drawl that reminded me of the Beverly Hillbillies TV show.

"Yes, we're here to see Detective Lieutenant Maybell," I said.

"Shore, hold on." He made a call and about two minutes later Maybell came out. He gave Bonnie the once over and asked us to come back. We followed him down narrow hallways to an office at the back and in.

We all sat and Maybell asked why he shouldn't arrest Bonnie. She looked panicky and I said, "First hear us out, then decide. Go ahead Bonnie tell him what you told us."

The girl went into the details of what happened that night and about finding the homeless shelter, she finished a few minutes later.

"Before we came here, Penny and I took Bonnie back to her motel to clean up, she was a little ripe from being in the sewers, so we know she was in the outdoors for the past few days."

Maybell sat back and gave Bonnie a stare, "Why

80

didn't you come to us about this first before Mr. Richards?"

"I don't know anyone here and I trust Mr. Richards. I've had a few bad experiences in the past with police."

"Yes, ah know. Ah found out a little about y'all after checking around and y'all have been hospitalized for having mental breaks. The police had to arrest you in a shopping center for acting crazy."

"They were mean to me, I can't help it if I have an imbalance that makes me a little paranoid at times."

"Three times according to ma sources. They say y'all weren't violent at all, but just confused. You taking y'all medications regular now?"

"I have been but I didn't have them yesterday. I took them when Jim and Penny took me to my motel, just in case."

"That's real good, they say it stabilizes y'all. Now this man you saw, y'all don't know him?"

"No, I never saw him before."

"Would y'all recognize him again?"

"I didn't see him very well the first two times, the first time it was dark and the second, he was too far away and was wearing sunglasses."

"Okay, we kin put ya in protective custody away from harm if y'all agree."

She looked to me, and then Penny then back to Maybell. "What would that entail?"

"Well ah kin put an officer on you jest until we find this man. How's that sound?"

"Can Mr. Richards watch me?"

I spoke, "Bonnie, I think it would be better with a police officer, they have a better grasp on stopping an attack on you. If I shoot someone, I'd be here filling out papers forever."

She cracked a smile and said, "I understand, okay I'll take the protection, just keep him away from me."

"Now jest a couple more questions. You said the man was punching the woman in the stomach?"

"It looked like it from where I was. I screamed when I realized or thought she was dead. He turned and saw me under the parking lot light. He came after me but I ran."

"The person you say you saw punching the woman, was actually stabbing the woman in the stomach."

I could see the look of shock on Bonnie's face. "I didn't see the knife, he had his back to me as he did it."

"Well the woman survived, possibly because of y'all

scream, he didn't git to finish her off."

He sat thinking and then said to me. "What do you think?"

"I still waiting on my man in the FBI to get back to me with anything on Val's background in her hometown. To see if she had a nasty boyfriend or ex who wanted her dead. I'll call to see if I can push them along."

"Well, that works for me. Keep me informed. As for you little lady, you are going to need to sit in y'all motel room with one of ma men watching. That goin' ta be a problem fer you?"

"No sir, that makes me feel a lot safer. Thank you."

"Well, we'll take care of this right off." He got on his phone and called someone to send a officer to see him.

After a few minutes an officer came to the door, it was Schmitt from the hospital. He acknowledged me and Penny.

"Is Blake Shelby back at the hospital?" I asked. He said he was.

Maybell explained what he wanted him to do and he said it would be his pleasure. He asked Bonnie to follow him and they went out after I gave Schmitt her car keys and telling him where the car was. Bonnie was out of ear shot and I quietly said not to let her drive. He agreed. I didn't want her taking off with the car.

83

They left and Maybell asked, "So now that she's out of the room, what do y'all really think?"

"I'm buying it for now, until I get all my info back. Do you have her stats that you came up with so I can look it over?"

"Shore do," he said and pulled a folder out of his desk and put it in front of me. "Y'all can take it, I have a copy."

"If she has mental problems, she may be making this all up. But I'm wondering about the man at the hospital, she couldn't have made him up. Penny said he came in and then when he saw her he turned quickly and went out. I saw him earlier. He may have a lot to do with this and he may be who Bonnie says she saw."

"Yep, and that's the only reason she's not in a cell. But if this man turns out to be a mistake, ah'm pulling her in."

*

Chapter 12

Maybell sat back and asked, "Either one of y'all could ID this guy?"

"I saw him in the mirror, briefly, but I could fill in what Penny saw," I said.

Penny smiled and spoke, "I could identify him if I saw him again, yes."

"Do you have a sketch artist?" I asked.

"We have a young woman who draws fer us. Want I should call her in?"

"If you want a face to put out for a BOLO it might be a good idea."

"Yep, that shore is a good idea, ah'll call her in."

He picked up his desk phone and made a call. He talked to someone and said to locate Steph and send her to his office with her sketchpad. He hung up and sat back.

Penny was shifting Willy in his bag, he was fussing.

"Maybe he wants to go outside for a whiz," I said quietly to her.

"Well, you take him out; I'm not picking up poop outside a cop shop." She gave me a look that said she was serious.

"Okay, hand him here," I said as she pulled the dog out of the bag and handed him to me. Maybell was chuckling at our predicament as I excused myself to go out.

"We do have pooper scooper laws here, do y'all want a baggie?" he said before I got out of the room.

Sunshine State Murders

"It would be a help. What have you got?"

He opened a lower drawer on his desk and pulled out a small wastebasket plastic bag and handed it to me. I knew how to pick-up and contain poop with a baggie, so I was now prepared. "Please don't bring it back in here," he said with a grin. I said I wouldn't.

I took Willy out and after about ten minutes of sniffing around, he did his business. I packed away his business in the bag and dropped it in an outside waste container by the door. I went back in to find a young woman with Penny, drawing the suspect. I sat next to her and watched the girl sketching the man, she was good.

"That looks like the man I saw in the restroom and coming out from the ICU. Good likeness."

Maybell was quietly sitting at his desk and then the girl held up the sketch for him to see.

"Nice lookin' man. Now we jest need to find him," he said and yelled to the door for someone named Forster. A few seconds later, a man came in and the girl handed him the sheet with the sketch.

"Forster, git this on the wire for a BOLO will ya?" Then he gave him the reason for arrest; suspicion of attempted murder and to proceed with caution.

The man nodded and went out. "Okay, we are one step up now." Maybell said and stood, thanking the girl, she left the room as Penny and I stood.

"Well, we are done here until we kin find the man, so thank ya kindly and I'll be in touch."

I shook Maybell's hand, then Penny and I left the office and out the front door to the parking lot.

I sat a minute before starting the car. "What's up?" Penny asked.

"Ah'm jest goin' ova the last week in ma mind"

"Stop that or I'll walk to the motel."

"Stop what, thinking or talking that way?"

"Both, jest drive, honeychile'"

I started the car still thinking about the events since we arrived here, hoping Earl gets some info for me so we can proceed. I turned the car in the direction of the hospital, Penny asked where we were going, I told her.

"Yep, we should check on Val and Blake. Good idea."

We arrived and went in to the ICU but Val wasn't there. I went back to the nurse's station and asked where she was.

"Mr. Richards, your publisher called and insisted on a private room. So they moved her just off the ward. Room 5, on the left down this hall."

"Thank you," I said and took Penny to the room. We entered and Blake jumped when I opened the door. "Don't shoot, it's just us."

"Mr. Richards, good to see y'all, it's been so quiet in here. Ah asked if they could bring in a TV, they's working on it."

"Well, my publisher is paying for it, go all out," I said with a smile. Penny went to Val and sat next to her.

"She's been drifting in and out," Blake said. "She hasn't said anything yet."

"It'll take time, but I'm sure she will."

My cell phone buzzed and I excused myself and went out into the lobby as I answered, it was Earl. "Got anything for me?"

"Well hello to you too," he replied.

"Sorry, hello, now what do you have?"

"I did some real digging and came up with some good dirt. First, your man in New York, Kenneth Lyle Parker, had a bookstore on the Avenue of the Americas no less, in Manhattan. Was there for about five years then a Barnes and Nobles opened just a stone's throw and put him out of business. He drifted for about a year from job to job and was being a bad boy according to the police reports. He was pulled in three times for spousal abuse, but the wife never pressed charges and he was cut loose. He finally packed up and moved to Palatka and set up shop again and has been laying low since. The wife, Linda, died two years ago from unknown causes; the coroner's report that I managed to get, said heart failure, nothing to point to him even though they investigated."

"I wonder if Ken's temper flared again when he had a few to drink and got mad because Val shot him down."

"Possible, now speaking of Val, that took me a bit more subterfuge to get her info. I found out where she lives and then did some looking. She lives in relative boredom in a house with her dog and cat. The neighbors say she was quiet and never bothered anyone."

"How did you talk to her neighbors?"

"I have people. They have people and those people are everywhere. I just made a couple calls and had some people inquire. I'm good."

"So you found nothing on her other than being boring?"

"Oh no, my suntan friend. I have more."

"I'm not suntan."

"All this time in Florida and no tan, that's unnatural."

"Never mind, just tell me what you found."

Sunshine State Murders

He laughed and paused. Then when I coughed he said, "Seems she had a rather scary boyfriend who didn't live with her but would treat her rather badly. One neighbor said it was he who caused the problems. She was the quiet one, and the abused one. Some lady who lived in the walk-up over Val's apartment, said she saw Val packing a lot of suitcases this last week and drove off."

"She ended up out here. I'll have to find out where her car is at and search it." I thought about Bonnie's car and Val's being still unattended. I'd have to go check on that soon.

"Any name or whereabouts of the boyfriend?"

"Yep, my pasty white friend, I do have that intel."

I waited, "So, what?"

"Sorry I was waiting for you to say you were ready to take my intel."

"My cell phone is recording this conversation; I'll replay it later for the intel. So speak."

"Okay, he's Steven Myerson, age 39, five-ten, good build from what I hear, brown-black hair, and mean tempered. He drives a late model Chevy Nova, license number 473KLM, and was last seen at her apartment just after Val split."

"That's good stuff. Thanks and if you find out anything more let me know."

He said he would and told me to get a tan, then hung up. I went to the nurse's station and asked for a pencil and paper. I ran the recording back to the information about Myerson and wrote it down. I called Maybell and told him about my call from Earl.

"That helps," he said after I relayed the plates and description.

"It sounds like Bonnie's description of the man chasing her. How is she doing?"

"Ma man is trying his best to keep her under wraps, she's a nervous one."

"Maybe I'll stop by later to try and calm her."

"Y'all do that or ah'll have Schmitt shoot her." I heard him laugh and hang up.

I went back to Val's room and told Penny and Blake what was said by Earl.

"So it's looking like this man is the one who attacked Val?"

"Seems that way now." I looked past Penny, towards Val; she had her eyes open wider now and was rubbing her nose. I pointed Penny to her and she went to the bedside followed by me.

"Val can you hear me?" Penny asked.

91

Val turned her head to Penny and smiled. "That's a good sign," I said.

"Val, can you tell me what happened to you?" I asked.

She was trying to clear her throat just as a nurse came in and said, "We saw that her vitals on the machine had elevated. She's awake now?"

"Yes, but she's not speaking."

The nurse went to her, checked her heartbeat and looked into her eyes. "Valerie, can you speak?"

Val was still trying to clear her throat. The nurse brought up a glass that she poured water in from a small pitcher and helped Val to drink some.

She stood holding the glass for Val and letting her drink a little more, then Val cleared her throat again and said, hoarsely, "Thank you."

*

Chapter 13

The nurse went to get the doctor, Penny stood next to Val like a mother hen, arranging her hair off her face. She looked tired and sweaty, but had a new vigor in her face, like she wanted to get up and go.

"Penny dear, can you do the beauty parlor thing later; I need to talk to her please," I said.

Penny smiled and stepped back, motioning to me with her hand to go right ahead. I went to Val's bedside and kissed her forehead. She smiled and said "Hi Jim."

"Hello Val, how are you feeling?"

"Not really well, thanks," she said still clearing her throat.

"Okay, if you can talk about it, can you tell us who did this to you?"

"I'm pretty sure who did it, that asshole boyfriend of mine, Steve Myerson."

I said under my breath, "Yes."

"What did you say?" Val asked.

"Not important, we got information that he may have done this, but we weren't totally sure. We have the police already looking for him. It will be a matter of time, but we'll get him."

"Good, now what happened to me? I mean after I argued with Steve."

"Well according to Bonnie Richner, he hit you on the back of the head with a rock and then stabbed you in the stomach with a knife, well, she didn't see him knife you but she said it looked liked blood coming from your in the stomach. The doctors said you were lucky that the knife didn't hit any serious organs. Your intestines have been put back together through surgery and they say you should be good as before. Now it's your head we were worried about."

"Other than a slight headache, I feel good. I'm still a little fuzzy with my vision but I can think straight." She thought for a minute then said, "Strange, Steve didn't even own a knife, or he never told me he did."

The doctor came in and asked if he could to get to Val. I stood back as he did his doctor business.

I turned to Penny and said, "I'm calling Maybell to tell him we got the right man for the attack." I went back out to the lobby and called.

He was pleased that we had confirmation of the attacker and said they were still looking and will update the warrant to attempted murder. I said I'd talk later and hung up. I went back to Val's room and Penny was next to her again, stroking her forehead with a wet towel. Val was sitting up better now and sipping from a straw in a cup. I presumed it was some kind of medicine.

She saw me and smiled, "Jim, come here and sit." She patted the side of the bed opposite Penny. I went to her, sat and took her free hand; it felt warm and soft.

"We were so worried about you. They said you were in a coma, we weren't sure if you were going to make it," I said.

"I had the strangest dreams, I can't really remember but I know they were strange. Where am I?"

"You're in Palatka General Hospital, in a private room thanks to Morty. He called and insisted that they put you in this room. See, you are special."

She laughed, it sounded good. Then she got a look on her face, "Where's Steve?"

"We don't know yet, they have an arrest warrant out for him. I'm sure they'll find him so don't worry. Besides you have protection." I turned to Blake and called him over. He came and stood next to me. "Val this is Officer Blake Shelby, your protector."

Val held out her hand to shake and Blake took it, turned red and said, "Pleasure to meet y'all ma'am."

"I prefer Miss, not ma'am, it makes me sound old." She laughed and Blake turned redder.

"It's a southern thang ma'am, er, Miss. We respect all

women and call them ma'am. But ah'll call you Miss now."

"Thank you, Blake. How old are you?"

If he got any redder I'd say he could pass for a tomato. I thought of another person who blushed easily, Lacey. But only when she was talking about sex.

"Ah'm 36 Miss Val."

"Hmm, I'm only two years older, do you like older women, Blake?"

"Val that's unfair to Blake. Be nice," I said.

"Damn being nice, I think Blake is cute."

Okay, Blake wobbled a little; I thought he was going to pass out from too much blood to the brain.

"Thank y'all, Miss Val, but I have a girlfriend."

"Damn, all the good ones are taken. Wait! Did you say Bonnie Richner saw my attack?"

"Yes, she did. That's how we figured Steve was the one who did it."

"Why was she watching me?"

"She said she was waiting for me to get back to the motel so she could talk to me about my books and saw you walk around the building, she later followed and saw Steve, hovering over you and blood on your stomach area."

"That's creepy, from that creepy girl. Where is she now."

"Under witness protection by the local police at her motel. She's safe. If she hadn't screamed you may have been dead, she stopped Steve, then he chased after her but she got away."

"Well as long as she didn't do this to me."

"Nope, she's in the clear. Now you need to get better so we can get you out of here."

"I'll try to heal fast, thank you."

The doctor came back in with some equipment to poke and probe Val and asked us to wait outside. Blake went with us, but stood by her door.

"I'm so glad she's better now," Penny said.

"I am too." I smiled at her comment. I went to the window in the waiting room looking out to the parking lot and saw our car; Willy was standing up barely being able to look out the window. Poor pup, we figured it was easier to leave him in the car than to shuffle him from Blake to Penny to me. He saw me and was jumping. I turned and saw Maybell coming through the doors followed by some woman. He saw us and came over.

Sunshine State Murders

"Jim this is our court reporter, she's goin'a take your friend's statement fer the record."

I said hello and Maybell asked if Val was presentable.

"She's being probed by the doctor but I'm sure you can go in."

He motioned for the woman to follow and went through the door. Penny and I sat and waited. Blake went in with Maybell and all was quiet now in the waiting room.

"This is so like you," Penny said.

"What did I do now?" I asked.

"Every time we get a nice event, murder happens."

"There was no murder."

"Well, it's only a matter of time."

I took her hand and kissed it.

"Don't try and get on my good side," she said.

"You have no good side my dear."

She huffed and whacked my arm; she hadn't done that in a long time. I smiled.

"I'm hungry, shall I call for a pizza?" I asked.

"I doubt they will deliver here, but you can try."

"We can share it with the nurses, that way they will let us."

I pulled my Palm TX and hooked up to the Google maps and found a pizza place, dialed from the information and placed my order. They said it would be about thirty minutes and I said that would be good and told them where we were. I hung up and said, "I ordered three. Enough for everyone."

"Good, now all is fine."

About forty minutes later, the pizza came and I put them on the nurse's station. They all went at the food like piranha, I barely got two pieces on a napkin before losing my hand and went to eat. Penny was munching on the first of three pieces she liberated from the attack. Maybell and his court reporter came out and I offered them pizza. Maybell laughed aloud and took a piece. The court reporter left after she said she would have the transcription later. Blake wasn't with Maybell.

"Where's Blake?" I asked.

"Where else would he be, guarding the woman."

I laughed silently and wondered if Val cared that Blake had a girlfriend. I finished my pizza, looked to

Sunshine State Murders

Maybell who had sat while eating his pizza and said, "I'm wondering if Myerson hasn't slipped the area now knowing we have Val and Bonnie being watched."

"I put out a statewide alert for him and notified the state police; we got his photo off his driver's license and posted it on the LEIN. Plus, with his plate number and car description, we'll get him."

"Good, this has been a strange week. I expected my book tour to be peaceful and make lots of money for my publisher, even though they don't send much of it to me. Val has been editing my books for almost a year and a half and knows me and my writings. I would have hated to lose her."

Blake came out and said, "Val's sleeping now. The doctor gave her something to help her rest."

"Rest? She's been in a coma for almost three days and he wants her to rest. Amazing." I said.

"Well this is good rest now." Maybell said and stood. "Ah'll let y'all know if'n we get word. Take care." Then he went off out the doors.

I turned to Blake and asked, "Did Val proposition you before she passed out?"

"She shore did that, Mr. Richards, but ah held her off," he said proudly.

*

Chapter 14

Penny and I were driving away from the hospital after being told by the doctor that Val would probably be out for the night. It was starting to get late, but I had one more stop.

"Where are we heading now?" Penny said from her side of the SUV.

"To go see Bonnie and make sure she's keeping out of trouble."

"Has she become your pet project now?"

"No, but if it weren't for me, she wouldn't have been here, and Val may have been worse than she was."

"How much worse, death?"

"Yes, and it would mean my curse is working. But she didn't die so that negates my curse."

"We aren't out of the woods yet," she said and giggled to herself.

We arrived at the motel and up to the door. I knocked and was met by officer Schmitt with a Colt 45 aimed at me. I guess southern cops liked Colts, it must be a cowboy thing.

"Oh sorry, Mr. Richard, ah was hopen' it would be the killer."

"Attempted killer, but that's beside the point, glad you are on the ball. Have you shot Bonnie yet?"

"Ah came close a couple times, that girl is a bit nuts."

"Where is she?"

"In the bathroom, don't ask me what she's doin', ah don't want to know." He turned back into the room and I entered followed by Penny carrying Willy.

I went to the bathroom door and called for her. She came flying out when she heard my voice.

"Jim, you came to see me?" she said almost bouncing.

"Calm down, I just came to tell you we know the attacker now. It's a nasty boyfriend of Val's, Steve Myerson, and the police are looking for him. Val is awake and talking now."

"Oh, fantastic. Does that mean he won't be coming after me now?"

"Well, it doesn't hurt to be careful, he's still out there."

"Yeah, but I want to get out of here. I have my car

back now and I really want to go back home."

"Well, I suppose that's your decision, but you still could be in danger. Are you sure you don't want protection?"

I could hear Schmitt mumble something about letting her leave. I didn't reply to him.

"I'm happy for the protection, but want to get out of here."

"If Myerson has your purse, doesn't he know where you live by your driver's license?"

"No, my license is in the visor of my car with my registration and insurance. I don't have it in my purse and there's not much in there to tell him where I live. Mostly I kept keys and woman stuff, you know make-up and things like that. I didn't have any important things in it. I don't have any credit cards, my credit sucks and there's nothing to point him to me living in Atlanta, so I'd like to go home."

I thought about it, getting her out of town would be nice; I had to call Maybell and see if she could take off.

"I'll talk to the detective in charge and see if we can let you go. Are you sure Myerson wouldn't be able to find you?"

"Why would he want me now? You have Val's statement that he was the one who attacked her, so he could care less about me now."

"True, but if they catch him they may need you to make a statement and to possibly identify him."

"As I said, I didn't see his face very well. I want to leave please; this has been more than I can take."

"I'll talk to Maybell and see what can be done." I looked to Schmitt, "Carry on, I'll be back."

I led Penny out of the motel room and went back to the car. I sat for a minute then pulled my cell phone. After a couple on rings, Maybell came on. I told him what Bonnie said.

"Shore, we kin let the lady loose. Good thing now, she's a pain in the ass. Tell her to go and send Schmitt back to the precinct."

"I'll do that. Thanks," I said then disconnected. I told Penny what I was going to do and got out of the car and went back to the room.

After a second, Schmitt opened the door, I told him and he smiled. Bonnie came up behind him and asked, "So, can I go?"

"We can help you put your suitcases in the car," I said with a grin.

Schmitt and I got her stuff in the car and I took her to the office to pay her bill. I took care of it since her money was in her purse and she thanked me. I gave her a hundred dollars to get her home and she was happy.

"Thank you so much Jim, I was very glad to meet you finally. I'll treasure our time together." She kissed me on the cheek and went to her car. She drove off as Schmitt and I stood watching her go.

"That was one psychotic woman," he said and went to his patrol car and drove off. Penny was still sitting in our rental watching all the activities.

"Is she really gone now?" she said hugging Willy.

"Yes, she's out of our lives now. So we can relax." I started the car and drove to our motel.

We arrived back at the motel and Penny changed into her swimsuit and went back out into the humid night to wet down swimming. I again sat watching her and Willy frolic in the pool. I was very surprised to see the same old man from the other motel a few days ago come out of a room and over to the pool, standing on the edge staring at Penny, then he turned to me.

"Oh yeah, you are the one with the gun. I admire the lady, is she really with you?"

I was trying not to laugh and said, "Yes, she is."

Just then the same overweight scary woman came out of his room and yelled for him to get back in. "Would you like to borrow my gun?" I asked.

Sunshine State Murders

"Don't tempt me," he said with a grin and went back to the room.

I sat in the drippingly wet night air and then told Penny I was going back to the air conditioning and watch TV. She said she'd be in shortly and I went off. The lights were off in the old man's room, I was afraid to even think what could be going on in there.

The next morning the sun was out and so was I. I sat on the chairs just off the pool and relaxed. It was good to know that Val was out of the woods and safe. Blake would never let anything happen to her and I was sure the police would find Myerson.

Penny came out a half hour later after she took a shower and dressed. "Sweetie, you're up early."

"Yep, I didn't sleep too well, between the AC and the humidity, it's hard to get comfortable. So I gave into the humidity and I'm enjoying the morning sun."

"Are we continuing on our tour?"

"As soon as I know Val is safe. Both from her attack and her attacker. He's still at large and needs to be found."

"Don't you think he'd be smart enough to run? Far from here?"

"True, maybe we need to move on also. I'll see what Val's condition is and maybe we can get out of here. Ah've had way too much of this."

"Shore nuff, babycakes," she said looking cute.

I stood and looked around the motel. I didn't see the old man, so either he murdered his wife or they left. I went back to the room followed by Penny and we got ourselves ready to go to the hospital to see Val.

Val was awake when we got there and she beamed when we came into the room. "Good morning you two."

Blake was sitting on his chair and stood after we came in, I said to relax, he did. I went to him and sat in the chair next to his as Penny went to Val, and I said to Blake, "Have you been here all night?"

"No, ah had relief over the night, ah jest got here about an hour ago."

"Has Val been behaving?"

"Shore nuff, she apologized for her attempt to seduce me yestaday."

"Great, she's a good person."

Val called me over; I went to sit on her bedside and took her hand.

"Jimmy, I am sorry for my actions yesterday, I was still groggy from the coma, I had a lapse in judgment when I tried to hit on Blake. He's a nice young man but not my type."

Sunshine State Murders

"Oh so you prefer crazy men who beat you?"

"That's unfair, Jim. He was a good man."

"I don't think any man who even touches a woman in anger is a good man. I don't excuse it. He will be caught and dealt with. And you need to get away from that kind of life. You are too good for him."

"Thank you Jim, I know I was stupid to put up with it for so long, but it's hard when one is dependent on someone who keeps putting me down and saying no one would have me but him. You start to doubt yourself."

"Well you are special and don't need that crap," Penny said.

"Easy for you to say, you have Jim."

"Oh believe me, he's no prize either."

They both laughed and I just sat there taking it.

*

Chapter 15

"Fine, I'm no prize, but I'm faithful." I defended.

"Yes you are, Sweetie. That's why I love you." Penny said and kissed my cheek as she leaned over Val.

"Hey guys, get a private room of your own." Val laughed.

"Val, talk to me, tell me about Myerson?" I asked.

She was silent for a moment, thinking. "We met in a grocery store of all places. He asked me which brand of deodorant was the best for over active males. I thought it was funny, and he was. He followed me around the store talking about various products and asking if they were any good. I finally told him to stop following me or at least take my phone number and go away. He took my phone number." She paused again as if she was trying to remember the day. "He called and we started to go out, first to a restaurant of course, then to a movie, then to bed. I was easy, and he took advantage. After a couple months of this he wanted to move in with me, but I didn't want to go that far and he didn't like it. We would fight about it and then make up. He did get a bit too rough every so often, especially when he drank and I would call the cops. But I couldn't have him go to jail, so I never pressed charges. I should have."

"Well, he's not going to hurt you again. You would be crazy not to press charges now. Besides, it's a criminal case of attempted murder, so he won't get off so easy with or without you," I said.

"I can't believe he would do this, he may have been rough but he didn't seem violent."

"Sometimes it's the quiet rough ones who surprise you," Penny said.

"Well, no matter what, I'm finished with him. He was crazy enough to track me down here and attack me. That's just sick."

"How did he track you down, what do you think?"

"I told my upstairs neighbor about you and how I was going to visit here for your book signing. I guess he found out from her."

"He's probably on the run now, if he knows what's good for him," I said.

"Yeah, well he may be good looking but he wasn't very smart. I often wondered just why I was even with him. We were so far apart mentally; I was way ahead of him in brainpower. He was just a pretty face and great body, but the upstairs apartment was very vacant."

"Opposites attract, they say," I said.

"That's stupid, and the people who say that are stupid."

"I didn't say it, I was just repeating it."

"I would never say you're stupid, Jimmy."

"Yeah, well he can be sometimes," Penny piped in. I gave her a stare and she said, "Sorry Sweetie, you aren't stupid, just a little dense."

"That's better." My cell phone buzzed and I excused myself and went out to the lobby. Caller ID said it was Maybell. "Hello, I hope you have good news."

"Well, ah kin tell you that State Police stopped Myerson over in Interlachen, they is bringing our boy back now."

"Great, may I sit in on the questioning?"

"As long as y'all behave yourself," he laughed and hung up.

I went back to the room and stood watching Penny and Val chattering to each other, having a good time. I wondered if Val would like to hear that her boyfriend was picked up or not. I took a leap.

"Val, just got word that Steve was picked up in some town called Interlachen by the State Police. They are bringing him in now. Is there anything you need to say that I can tell the detectives?"

Val looked a bit shocked then her expression changed, "Fry the bastard. He can rot in jail for all I care."

"Well, I can tell them that, but you have nothing else to say about what happened that night?"

She thought for a moment then said, "We argued, he was mad about my getting away from him, I was finished with him and told him so. I turned to go to my room and that's the last thing I remember until waking here to see your ugly mug," she said with a smirk.

"Well, it was good that you saw me and not St. Peter. I'm going to watch them interrogate Steve and I'll fill you in later." I looked to Penny and asked, 'Do you want to go watch or stay here?"

Penny looked to Val, and paused. Val said, "Go, and give me the dirt when you get back."

Penny smiled and said, "I'll make sure they fit him with a nice orange jumper." She leaned to Val and kissed her on the forehead, "Stay safe," she said and we left.

We drove over to Palatka precinct and parked, then went in the building to find Lieutenant Maybell in his office. He waved us in. We sat.

"Is he in yet?" I asked.

"They're booking him now, and will have him in interrogation shortly," Maybell said.

"Has he said anything to the arresting officers?"

"Nope, he has been more than unhelpful to the officers. He just stayed uncooperative. That's all right, ah'll break him."

"Val didn't have much more to say about it from her bed. I'm sure you can break him."

"Mr. Richards, ah have a good background in beating a suspect." He paused, "Ah gave a call to your friend Lieutenant Lynn Carter out in Vegas. She speaks highly of you and your abilities to get the case solved. Ah don't know if'n ah should believe her, but ah don't want to disrespect a fellow officer. Ah'm letting you sit in on the interrogation, you may be helpful. Ah hope." He smiled just as an officer came to his door and said Myerson was in interrogation room two.

"Lieutenant, why did you call Lynn?"

"Well, ah suspect everyone in an attempted murder, so ah had to check y'all out. I knew y'all wrote books on crime and y'all are a P.I., but I still had to check. Y'all came through with flying colors."

"I'm glad to hear that. Are you going to question him right away or let him sweat?" I asked.

He laughed and said, "Ah had the guard turn up the temperature in the room. He'll be sweating like a Southern hog on a summer day." He laughed again and stood. Penny and I stood and followed him to the rooms. He directed Penny to observation and pointed me to the door to where I could see Myerson sitting looking uncomfortable.

Sunshine State Murders

Maybell called over to the guard and told him to turn up the air conditioner full in the room. He turned to me and said, "That should get his nipples tight."

We stood outside the room for a few minutes talking about my book tour then Maybell said it's time to go defrost the suspect. We went in and Maybell pointed me to a chair, he sat across from Myerson and smiled.

"How y'all doing sport? Ah'm Detective Lieutenant Maybell, do y'all object to this conversation being recorded?"

Myerson blinked a few times and quietly said no. I could see how Val could go for a guy like him. He was handsome and rough looking, a real ladies' man.

"I understand y'all been given your rights, so we will proceed." Maybell sat back and said, "Steve, can y'all tell us jest what happened the other night when Valerie Brookside was attacked?"

Myerson sat silently, looking to the tabletop and his clenched hands. "I didn't hurt Val, I loved her."

"Y'all love her so much to take a rock to her head and then stab her in the gut six times?"

"Stabbed?" He looked shocked. "I didn't stab her, okay I admit I hit her with the rock, but I didn't stab her? God, I'm not a killer."

Bob Moats

"Y'all could have killed her with the rock ya know."

"Okay, I left the place after I hit her, but I came back to see if she was alright."

"Y'all hit her, fled and then came back to see if y'all finished the job?"

"No, we argued and she made me so mad, when she turned to walk away from me, I picked up a rock and hit her. She fell and didn't move, I was scared and ran, but I thought maybe she was just hurt, so I came back to see if I could help her. When I got back I could see Val was bleeding from her stomach. I heard someone behind me and turned, it was some woman standing in the bushes near by, I went to her and she screamed. I just wanted explain that I didn't do it, but she ran."

I thought that must have been the scream we heard that night.

"I got scared again when I heard voices coming, so I ran after the woman. She ran for a while then I gave up trying to stop her to find out what she saw. I didn't want to be arrested and she was a witness."

"Did you happen to notice any blood on the mystery woman?" I asked.

He paused a moment thinking, "You know I think she had a fancy blouse with red dots on it. It was a light colored blouse and the red splotches made it look odd. Maybe it was blood, I can't say."

115

I was now wondering if Steve was a good liar or he saw more than Bonnie was telling. I now worried that we let her go.

"Could you identify this woman?" I asked.

"It was dark and she kept her head low, but I think I could."

I looked to Maybell, "We may need to bring Bonnie back."

   *

Chapter 16

They put Myerson in a cell and I went to Penny in observation. Maybell went off to put an APB out for Bonnie. I was ·smart enough to write down Bonnie's license plate number just in case.

"So are we back to Bonnie being the attempted murderer?" Penny asked.

"It may be. Unless Stevie boy is lying to cover his ass. Bonnie could have been telling the truth but we need to get the two of them together and let them fight it out."

"So we now don't have a definite answer for the attack?"

"Well, it looks that way. I'm betting on Steve. Although Val did say he wasn't the killer type, but you never know. Bonnie seems a little off, you should know that, she did threaten you."

"Since I've been with you, I've had a lot of threats. I'm getting used to them by now. I just blow them off."

"Well, be careful which one's you blow off. I don't want you hurt or dead."

"I'll let you know when I get a threat that worries me."

We sat quietly for a few minutes then I said, "Let's get out of here and go let Willy take a crap on the police lawn."

We were back in the hospital and went to find Val asleep; Penny gently woke her. Penny then sat and told her all about the interview; Val looked a bit relieved that Steve wasn't trying to kill her.

"Don't write him off yet, he could have lied about Bonnie's involvement," I said.

"I know, I've read your books, nothing is what it seems."

"You learn well, grasshopper," I said.

Blake returned from the men's room and went back to his chair.

117

Sunshine State Murders

"We have the main suspect in custody, are they still having you watch Val?" I asked him.

"I jest sit and watch so long as they say. Ah'm in no hurry to go back to road duty."

"I can see that, maybe they forgot about you."

"That be right good with me," he said with a big grin.

"Jimmy, how long am I going to be in this place?" Val asked.

"I can talk to the doc and see." I went out of the room and asked at the nurse's station where Val's doctor was. She said he was in surgery, but she'd let him know I was looking for him. I asked, "Do you think Val is ready for release?"

"She's looking good, I think she may be released shortly."

I thanked her and went to the lobby and pulled my cell phone, I called Earl.

"Hey, I need another favor," I said when he answered.

"Why does that not surprise me?" he said.

"I need some info on a woman, name's Bonnie Richner. License plate number 893ABA out of Georgia.

See what dirt you can come up with. Thanks, now is the office still standing?"

"Trapper is trying to sell shares in the place, but having no takers. Buck has gone over to the dark side and is recruiting criminals being released from prison to work for him and plotting to take over Las Vegas. Lacey is starting an escort service and hiring hookers recommended by Trapper. Other than that, all is just quiet out here."

"Good, all is normal then."

"Yep it is. I'm wondering if coming out here was a good idea. I've been way too busy with cases and I think we need you back here."

"Soon, I may cut my tour short if this case here doesn't get solved soon."

"Why don't you just let the police take care of it?"

"The attack was committed on a friend, I don't leave until we figure who did it to her."

"Well, I hope you finish it up soon, Lacey is getting a bit too bossy without you here."

"Put up with it, she's looking out for the firm's best interests."

"Yeah, well I may have to put her down if she doesn't quit yelling at me about leaving the back door open."

"Well, stop it, you never know who may wander in."

"I like fresh air and we have no windows in this place. Speaking of that, my sharing an office with Will is getting a bit tense. I can't talk to a client if he's sitting there snickering. I talked to everyone and we agree that we need a bigger office. Buck's guards are all over the place, they need a room for their own, and I need a private office. I swear I was ready to move into the rest room the other day."

"Well, you guys work on it, I'm fine with a bigger building, just get me one with windows in my office and don't put me out back. Now get me the intel on Bonnie, please, thank you." We finished and I hung up.

I went back to the room and told Val that the doctor would get back to me later. She was squirming and said she wanted out.

"I may just do a jail break if the doctor doesn't release me soon," she said.

"We'll know today, and I'm sure you will be let loose. Where do you plan on going now? You left your apartment and have no place here to stay since we took your stuff from your motel room and closed that down."

"I still have my apartment, I just moved a few clothes out so Steve would think I was gone. I can go back there anytime. Mrs. Potrice upstairs has been watching the place for me. I'm no dummy."

"I know you aren't, I'm glad you still have your place. What city is it in by the way."

"I live in White Springs, just north of Lake City. Not a huge town but it's comfortable. By the way, where is my car?"

"I asked for one of the police to bring it to our present motel and parked it. I check on it to make sure it's safe. We need to get you a room when they let you out, but you'll need to stay around until they get the case settled."

"That would be fine, but I don't have enough money to stay in a motel for very long."

"Don't worry, I'll foot the bill and then charge it to Morty. He's paying for your room here, if you didn't dislike this place so much you could just stay here on him."

She laughed, "I want to go home right now, I've had it with this place."

Penny said, "We can get you a room next to us at our motel and go swimming, oh, sorry, I forgot about your wounds."

"Damn, I almost forgot about them too. Well, I can sit and watch you swim. I'll keep Jim company."

My cell phone buzzed and I excused myself. I went to the lobby and answered, it was Maybell.

Sunshine State Murders

"That plate number y'all gave us came up not in Atlanta. It's registered to Bonnie, but in Valdosta, Georgia, jest north of the state line. A whole lot closer than Atlanta. Ah got state police watching fer her at the state line. If'n she sticks to the main roads they should find her. Did she know you took her plate number?"

"I don't think so, I wrote it down while she was packing. Well, she's lied a couple times now that we know of, I'm changing my vote for her being the attacker. But if you ask my wife, I have been known to be wrong."

"Most wives say their husbands are wrong most the time. Ah'll let you know what we find."

He hung up and I called Earl back to give him the new info on Bonnie's hometown.

I told Earl about the new details and then Earl said, "I just got off the phone with a friend in the, well, you don't want to know, he already told me about Valdosta. It also seems that Bonnie has also split out from a mental hospital and they are looking for her."

"Why?"

"She has a violent temper and has attacked a number of people in the recent past. The law sent her in for observation as part of her sentence, but she walked out of the hospital they were giving her tests at. She packed a few things and left town. She violated her terms of incarceration and they have a warrant out for her."

"Well then I don't think she would go back to her

town if they want her bad enough. So she's out there somewhere, waiting for what? We're looking for her for the attack on my friend, she wouldn't hide around here. Well, if you find out anything more, let me know."

"Will do, oh, and we think we found a nice building just down the road from here. A former law office, with sweet private offices for all of us."

"You guys work fast, if the rent is good, go for it, but I get the best office, you hear? Or I'll be kicking out a few people."

"We have the perfect office for you, you'll love it."

"Why does that worry me. You better put me in a good room."

"You got it, talk later," he said then hung up.

I called Maybell back, this was getting old. "Hi, I have new information on Bonnie; she's an escaped felon and has warrants out for her."

"Boy howdie, when y'all wrong, y'all really wrong. If'n she's wanted back in Valdosta, she probably won't go back there."

"My thoughts exactly. Now we just have to figure where on earth would she go?"

*

Chapter 17

"Tell me everything you found out about her," Maybell asked as I sat back in his office. I had told Penny that I was needed by Maybell and it would be better if she stayed with Val. She agreed reluctantly and stayed.

"Well, it seems she has a violent temper and was arrested a couple times for attacking people. They sentenced her to psychological testing and she escaped from the hospital. All I know is she showed up here to get my signature on her books. I don't know whether to be pleased or repulsed that an escaped felon is a fan."

Maybell laughed and said, "Well, we'll find her. We got everyone looking fer her fer about one hundred miles around us. If'n she is running, she betta hide well."

"Is Myerson being more cooperative?"

"He's staying mum on the subject. He knows that Richner is out thar somewhere, and it's a matter of time afore we find her, but he'll still be in for the hit to the head."

"So assault is what you'll get him for?"

"Can't prove he intended to kill her, he just struck and ran. He kin claim a conscience by coming back, finding Richner and then ran agin. He'll have ta prove himself in court."

"Will Val have to hang around here?"

"It probably will have ta be, but maybe we kin just take her deposition and let her get on with her life."

"I think that would make her happy, she's going crazy in the hospital. I'm getting a little crazy myself, all this going on and I have a tour to complete. My publisher hasn't called yet but he will."

"Tell the man you got the makin's for a good book." Maybell laughed.

"I hate to say it but I already thought about that. May I use your name?"

"Jest spell it right."

"If the doc says it's all right for Val to leave the hospital, I'm going to put her up in our motel, but I think we need to move on. Change of scene will do everyone good."

"I'll make y'all a deal, you kin move on, but if'n things change back here, y'all come back."

"We can do that. The plan was to go to Orlando and then fly out to Washington, D.C. but we can hang around Orlando for a spell, to give you time to find Richner."

"That'll work fer me. Jest let me know where y'all are if'n I need ya."

Sunshine State Murders

"Deal."

I was back in the hospital and talked to the doctor and he said, "As long as Val doesn't complain or have pain, I can let her go as long as she is careful, so she didn't open up her wounds."

I said, "I'll watch her carefully. We need to get her out of here, and back to her life." Hopefully, without the craziness of Myerson, I thought.

"I hope it all goes well for her. Take care." He went off and I went to Val's room and found Penny still sitting, talking.

"Val, I have some bad news," I said.

She got a distressed look on her face. "The bad news is that people are going to miss you here. The good news is, you can leave. But only if you take it easy and not open up your wounds."

"Hell, you can put me in a wheelchair and roll me out, I'll not make a fuss. I just want to get out of here."

"Well, you can, so if Penny can help you to get dressed, carefully, we can check you out."

"I'm ready if you are," she said to Penny.

I went to Blake and said, "Maybell said for you to report back to road patrol, sorry."

"Damn, ah was hopin for a little more time, oh well." He stood and we went out of the room so Val could get dressed. Two of the nurses came in to help get her ready to leave. The head nurse came to me and said they needed to take care of the bill. I was at a loss for an answer.

"Let me call my publisher and see what we need to do to take care of this."

"We need a medical card or credit card either one, we accept."

"I'll tell him, thanks." She went off and I pulled my phone and went to the lobby. Blake said good bye and left.

"Morty, Jim Richards here," I said as soon as he answered.

"Jim how is my star editor, she needs to get back to work. Manuscripts are piling."

"Well the hospital is releasing her now and we will get her settled into a motel room, I'll see that she gets on her laptop and sends you the edits. Don't worry. Now the hospital needs some info for payment, you did agree to pay for her expenses."

"Crap, I did didn't I?"

"Yes you did, so I'll put you on with the people who will take care of that and then Val can get out of here, okay?"

"Alright, give them the number of accounting and I'll call to authorize it. So she's doing good now?"

"Better, but she still has gut wounds that need healing, as long as she doesn't do anything strenuous she'll be fine."

"Did they catch the person who did this?"

"Well, they got one of them."

"One?"

"It seems to be a conspiracy and it will make a great book, I'll send you a proposal and a draft. You'll love it, but it's not over yet so I'll have to update it as we find out more."

"Great, I'll look forward to it. Talk later, okay?"

"Sure, later," I said then disconnected the call. I gave the head nurse the info for the bill and she said she'd talk to admissions. I thanked her and went back to the room.

"Is everyone decent?" I called out before entering.

"Yep, we're ready." Penny called to me. I went in and found Val standing, dressed and the nurses fussing over her. One nurse went to get a wheelchair and brought it back to have her sit. I took command of the chair and wheeled her out. We had to stop at the nurse's station to sign some papers and then we went to the outside doors

Bob Moats

from the ICU.

We hit the front entrance of the hospital and the humidity and sunshine hit us. Val said, "Damn, that feels good."

I told Penny to wait with Val while I went to get the car.

"Are you feeling alright?" Penny asked Val while they waited.

"I'm doing good, there is a little pressure but it doesn't hurt. It's good to get fresh air again."

I pulled up and the nurse who came with us helped Penny to get Val up and into the SUV. I came around and held the wheel chair as they guided her carefully into the back seat.

When they had her in and buckled, the nurse took the chair back and said good-bye. I got back in and drove to our motel. I pulled into the parking and helped get Val out and into our room to sit. I went to the office and got another room, luckily they had one next to ours. I went back and told Val about the room and we guided her to it.

She sat on an easy chair as I brought her luggage from our room. She looked down to see Willy bouncing around her feet, she smiled and reached down for him. The two of them sat quietly as Penny was organizing her things from her luggage.

"Okay Val, you need to get to work," I said as I

pulled her laptop from it's case and set it up on the desk by the front window.

She laughed and said, "Morty threatened me didn't he?"

"Well, he did mention that your work was piling up. So, there is wi-fi here that you can upload the edits to Morty and I'll check in on you to make sure you are doing the job."

"Thanks, you are a pal." She stood slowly and winched; I said to go slow and helped. She went to the desk and sat, turning on the laptop and waited for it to boot up. Penny sat on the easy chair and relaxed.

"I'll take Willy out for a poop run," I said and went out.

Two hours later, Penny came out of Val's room where she was resting and reading a manuscript that Val had in her luggage. I was out by the pool sitting on the picnic table working at my laptop on my story about Earl's adventure. Willy was sleeping under the table on his leash. Penny plopped down next to me.

"Are we going on with the tour now?"

"Maybell said we could, but we had to be ready to come back in case we're needed. If they find Bonnie. I'm hoping it's soon so we can all get on with our lives."

"Where do you think Bonnie went off to?"

"I haven't the foggiest idea. She can't go back home, they have a warrant for her there. She can't stay around here, they have a warrant for her here. I almost feel sorry for her, but not much."

"You are just such a softy aren't you?" Penny laughed.

"I feel for the underdogs and downtrodden. I'd never be a good prosecuting attorney; I'd feel too sorry for the bad guys."

"But you'd be a poor defense attorney; you want to put all the crazies away. You may say you feel for the bad guys, but you really would like to have them all shipped off the planet. I know you."

"Fine, just sit there and watch me as I work," I said.

What I didn't know was that someone else was watching me also.

*

Chapter 18

After we all had a good night's sleep, we spent the entire next day just working on our laptops and writing, either edits or novels. Penny relaxed around the pool with Willy. The old man came out to say hi, just before his wife screamed for him to get back in the room. I decided to wait one more day before traveling further on our tour. I had called Morty and told him we would be in Orlando in two days; and to arrange to restart the tour then.

Val was feeling much better being out of the hospital and she said she was healing well. I wasn't going to examine the wounds, so I took her at her words. She wanted to go along with us to the next bookstore stop, I told her that was good with me.

"Actually, I needed this rest," Val said. "My life was a rut of editing and putting up with Mr. Macho, and he wasn't a very good thing in my life. I realized that about three months ago, just after the first time he started to beat on me. I'm finally getting my head together and getting away from him. Or so I hope. I also hope he rots in jail."

"They may only find him guilty of assault, depends on the courts. He may do some jail time but he will be getting out eventually," I said.

We were all in our room relaxing, talking about what we would be doing for the next few days. Morty had called again and said we were scheduled to appear at a bookstore in Orlando the day after tomorrow. He gave me the details and I wrote them down. Val and Penny were relaxing when someone knocked at the door to our room. I went to it, opened the door and was shocked to see Steve.

I had my Glock out of it's holster before he could even blink and he gave me a startled look.

"What the hell are you doing here?" I demanded.

"I was released on bail this morning, for assault, not a major crime my attorney argued. There was no proof I was trying to kill Val, so the judge let me out on bail. I'm out until the trial and I wanted to tell Val I was sorry."

"How did you find us?"

"I went to the hospital and they said Val was released and they wouldn't tell me where she went to. I figured she was staying at a motel so I went to every motel I could find until I saw her car here, in front of this room. I took a chance and knocked."

"I'm only going to say this once, you can either go away alive or carried away with a bullet, it's up to you," I said.

"I don't want to harm Val, I just want to apologize."

"I'll give her the message, now get lost."

I could hear Val behind me as she approached the door, "Steve, I'll accept your apology but I don't want to ever see you again. I will have Jim shoot you if you ever come near me again. I'll get my own gun if Jim isn't around and shoot you myself. Now please go."

He looked wounded and didn't say anything. "Are you going to say good-bye or just stand there?" I asked.

"I'm sorry," he said quietly and went to his car as I watched him leave.

I closed the door and turned to see Val, she had tears in her eyes and then hugged me. "I was never so frightened until that moment. I just didn't think I could be so affected by all this. I need to lay down, please."

"Val, take a breath and I'll escort you to your room." She smiled and then we went out and to her door, followed by Penny. Val put the key in and I checked the room, just for the hell of it. She went to the bed and laid down; Penny said to me that she would stay with her.

"That would be good. You have your .38 in your purse?"

"Of course, I never leave home without it," she said with a smirk. I kissed her, went back to our room and picked up Willy who was bouncing around at my feet. I grabbed my laptop case and took it and Willy out to the picnic table. I put Willy on his leash and tied it to the table leg, then sat. I pulled out my laptop and booted it up.

I heard a door open and the old man came back out and to the pool. He stood at the edge and looked around. I smiled and said, "She's resting in the room, sorry."

134

Bob Moats

He gave me a small smile and then leaned forward, splashing into the pool. I was surprised and waited for him to come up, he didn't. I jumped up and went to the edge where he went in and saw him just floating at the bottom. I pulled off my loafers, shirt and gun then dove in. I got down to him and pulled him up to the surface and over to the edge of the pool. I was yelling for Penny who heard me through the open window of Val's room.

She came to the door and saw me holding on to the old man and came running.

"Grab his shirt and hold him until I get out."

She held on to the man as I climbed up and then reached down to pull him up and out. I spread him out on the lawn and checked his pulse; he was alive. I patted his face a few times and called to him. He stirred, then opened his eyes.

"Are you St. Peter?" he asked.

I had to smile and said, "Nope, I'm the guy with the gun."

"Crap, I wanted to die. Why did you have to save me?"

"It's just how I am; I don't like to see people kill themselves."

Penny asked if she should call an EMT. I told her to wait.

"Why did you want to kill yourself? I asked.

"Delores is dead."

"Who's Delores?"

"My wife, the screaming shrew," he said with a smile.

"Why is she dead?" I said as I looked to his room, the door still opened.

"I killed her. She drove me to it, now because you saved me, I'll go to prison. I don't think I'd like that."

I looked to Penny and asked her to go look in the room. She went to the door I pointed to and slowly walked in. A couple seconds later, she came back out, she wasn't smiling.

"I told you there would be a death. She's just lying on the bed, no sign of blood."

The old man spoke from the ground, "That's because I poisoned her. Put it in her scotch and soda, rat poison. She was a rat. A bitchy rat, who didn't deserve to live."

I helped him up to a sitting position as I asked Penny quietly to call Maybell. She went off the side and called on my cell phone that I told her was in my shirt pocket. I had put the shirt, Glock and my shoes on the ground by the pool before I jumped in. I picked up my Glock and put it back in the holster on my belt, then put the shirt back on. The old man just sat there looking miserable.

Penny came back and said Maybell was coming.

The old man said, "Let me jump back in the pool please."

"I don't want to turn you over to the police, but I can't let you kill yourself."

An hour later, Maybell and his crew were examining the old man's room. The county coroner had removed the body and went off. The old man was sitting quietly on a lawn chair just outside the room. I was feeling sorry for him.

I pulled Maybell aside and explained the events of what I had witnessed the couple times I had contact with the man and how his wife was.

"Well, ah have seen a number of men who killed their bitchy wives. Heat gits to them down here and they'll do bad things. He may have a case for abuse, but that's up to the court."

I said I'd vouch for him, I saw what she was like.

Another half hour later, everyone was gone. The yellow police tape across the door of the old man's room flapped in the mild wind now coming in, bringing more humidity with it. Penny and I sat on the chairs by the pool just sitting quietly thinking about the events of the day. We were holding hands and she looked to me, "Do you ever think about poisoning me?" she said with her evil little smile.

"No, of course not, but I'm sure there have been times you wanted to do me in. Especially for my insurance, just make it look like an accident."

"I would never kill you, I have no time or desire to retrain a new husband. Or the desire to look for one. Most men are just a waste of life, or so stuck into their own world to be able to share it with a woman."

"That's a little cynical isn't it?"

"Me, cynical? Hardly. I'm realistic about life. It's hard nowdays to live a life like we had years ago. All the technology has moved us into a world of being alone with faceless people on the internet."

"Yep, cynical. I think there are still good people out there. This old man wasn't bad, he killed his wife out of survival. His own survival. The few times I had seen her, I probably would have poisoned her too."

The door to Val's room opened and she stood looking bleary eyed, then came to us. "I slept well, did I miss anything?"

I could feel Penny quietly laughing.

*

Chapter 19

Penny wanted to tell the story, so I let her. Val was sitting on a chair taking in all the dirt and looking occasionally to the yellow tape on the room.

"I always miss the good stuff," Val said. "Oh sorry, that wasn't good that the woman died, just a good story."

"It will go in my book, when I write about this adventure," I said with a laugh.

"Just leave me out of it," Val said.

"How can I write about all this without you?"

"You can use a fake name. Call me Dallas Glitzkiss, how about that?"

"Where did you get a name like that?"

"It just came to me, or I heard it somewhere. Maybe on Facebook. Whatever, Don't use me, I'll be embarrassed."

"I'd be embarrassed being called Dallas Glitzkiss. I'll think of a less obnoxious name." My cell phone buzzed annoyingly. I stood and went off the side and answered, it was Maybell.

Sunshine State Murders

"Well the old man won't be going ta trial," he said.

"Why?"

"He jest passed away, in his cell."

"You guys didn't beat him, did you?"

"Not even funny."

"Sorry, what happened?"

"The doc who handles our autopsies was called and said he thinks it was jest old age."

"How old was he?"

"Driver's license said eighty-nine. He was due and he won't be going to prison. Ah think that's better fer him. We found his next a kin, they's coming to identify the bodies, and collect their things."

"Well, it's sad that he died, but better for him. Changing the subject, any word on Bonnie?"

"Nope, she's dust in the wind."

"Kansas?"

"Now why would she be in Kansas?"

"No, the band Kansas, Dust in the Wind. A song they recorded."

"Y'all are a little strange, ya know."

"I've been told that many times by my wife."

"Well, listen to her," he said with a laugh and hung up.

I went back to the women and related what Maybell said.

"Poor man, but at least he won't go to prison," Penny said.

"Any word on Bonnie?" Val asked.

"He said she was dust in the wind."

"Kansas?" Val said.

"See, that's just what I said. He has no idea where she is from his statement. I'm sure she's hiding out in the swamps."

Val laughed, "She doesn't want to hide out there. The gators will get her."

"Okay, we need to plot our trip to Orlando. Morty said I am signing the day after tomorrow. So we need to travel fast."

"I can drive some of the time," Penny said.

"I have no problem with that, do you feel well enough to travel, Val?"

"I'm ready to get out of this town as soon as possible. This place is creepy."

"I thought it has a quaint charm," I said.

"If you like being attacked, sure."

"Are either of you hungry?" I asked.

"I am," Penny spoke.

"I could eat something. What do you have in mind?"

"Well I don't know if they have Sonics down here, do they?"

"Closest ones are either Daytona Beach or Ocala, but they both are too far to get a quick burger. We do have two Burger Kings though," Val said.

"Ah, that sounds good to me, if you two don't care for any more seafood," I said with a smile.

"I'm good with it," Penny said and she stood taking Willy with her to the room after saying she had to use the bathroom.

I sat with Val, she looked to me and said, "Is Steve going to leave me alone?"

"He better, if he knows what's good for him. I haven't shot anyone in a long while, so maybe he will make my day."

I stood and helped Val up and we went to the SUV when I saw Penny come back out of our room. What I didn't see was someone watching us.

Two hours later, we were back in our rooms packing our things so we could be ready to leave early in the morning. I had called Maybell to see if there was any reason we should stay, he laughed and said to get out of town as fast as we could. I told him about Myerson's visit to our room, I forgot to mention it when they picked up the old man, and he said he would have a man watch him. He knew where Myerson was staying, it was mandatory that he let the court know where he was at. I said that was good, he didn't seem threatening but he had a temper according to Val.

We were packed and I said for our last night in Palatka we could go to the Crossroad Saloon, just to celebrate us getting out of town. Val agreed hesitantly but said it was good with her. I pulled my cell phone and dug out the card Blake Shelby gave me with his cell number in case of emergency. I called him and he came on.

"Blake, this is Jim Richards, how you doing?"

"Ah'm good, whatcha y'all need?"

"We're planning on going to the Crossroads Saloon, would you like to escort us?"

Sunshine State Murders

"Ah'd be happy too. Where y'all at now."

I told him and he said he would be by shortly. I hung up and told Penny that I called our favorite officer.

About a half hour later, Blake showed up all dressed like he was going to a country bar, boots, jeans and cowboy shirt. I stifled a laugh but he did look nice in the outfit.

"Ah'm ready fer anything," He said with a smile.

"Where do you carry your gun?" Penny asked.

He smiled and pulled up one of his pant legs and there was his weapon strapped to his leg just inside the cowboy boot.

We all went out to our cars and I followed Blake back to the saloon. We went in and Blake was greeted by a number of people, I knew we were safe.

We partied and danced, Val did so carefully. Blake was being extra careful with her, I was glad for that. He sat close by so none of the men would bother her. She didn't mind, Blake may have been younger but he was good looking.

I had to watch the women so they didn't get too drunk. I wasn't going to have to be the bad guy but I didn't need a drunk Penny. She was hard enough to handle sober.

Blake knew the band and introduced us to them, Val

was feeling good and asked if she could sing with them. The band's leader, Butch, said she was more than welcome to and asked Penny if she wanted to also. Penny was bouncing and then the band got back up and introduced the women.

"Hey all, we have a celebrity with us tonight. Talk show host, or I should say former talk show host Penny Wickens and her friend Val Brookside. They are going to sing for you so let's give them a big hand."

The crowd went loud, the women went to the stage and the band started up the song they agreed on before starting. They sang Shania Twain's "Any Man of Mine" and it didn't sound too bad. They flubbed a few lines but the crowd loved it, laughed and sang along. They finished and Val was helped off the stage by Blake. She fell into his arms and hugged him. I could see his face going red, then he wrapped his arms around her and gave her a squeeze. She flinched and Blake remembered her wounds and backed off. Val grabbed on to him, pulled him back and said something in his ear. He turned even redder.

We were relaxing when Ken Parker came in and saw us. He came over and I asked him to join us.

"Ken, how are you doing?" I asked.

"I'm good, had a great night in the store, and sold a few more of your books. People all wanted to be there but had things to do. You should schedule another signing."

"You'll have to talk to my publisher about that. He doesn't like me arranging my own signings, he can't make

145

money if I go off on my own," I said with a laugh.

Val was in the ladies' room when Ken came in and sat with us, she looked a little surprised to see him. She sat away from him and latched on to Blake. I could see Ken's neck tighten up and wondered why. Then I remembered that he hit on Val last time we were here, so he was reacting to what he saw.

Ken asked me if we had the girl caught yet. I said "She's running from two warrants, but we will catch her yet."

"I can't believe she did this, it's tragic."

I said it was.

It was getting late and we decided to call it a night, we had to leave early so I led our little crew out of the bar. Ken stood when we left but stayed. I told him I'd talk to my publisher about doing another signing, I was liking the town and wanted to come back.

We got to our cars and Val said that she was having Blake drive her back. I figured she was a big girl; I worried more about Blake than her. She yelled to me before she got into his car and said they were going to get a burger. I said not to stay out too long.

Penny laughed and said, "Blake better be careful. Shall we go back and do what Val may be doing later."

"Hey, Blake is an honorable man," I said. We drove back and into our room, Willy wasn't happy being left

146

alone and I took him out for a whiz, then back in to hit the sheets.

Early the next morning, I was packing the car and then went to Val's room and knocked. I was surprised when Blake answered the door looking very sheepish.

*

Chapter 20

"Uh.. good morning Mr. Richards," he said with a red face.

"Relax Blake, I'm not judging anything. You're a big boy now."

He quietly laughed and said, "She is jest one hell of a woman."

"Yes, I imagine. Now what's the story, I mean is she still going with us or staying?"

"Oh, she wants ta still go, but ah'm going to drive her if'n y'all don't mind."

"No, that's fine as long as you keep up with us. What about your car?"

"Ah took it home early this morning and packed a few things then ah had a patrol car drive me back. Ah called my Lieutenant and took a leave of absence. He said that was fine with him."

"Well, this will work for me, you get to protect her and I don't have to worry about her safety. Should I be worried about your safety?" I said with a grin.

"Oh no, Ah'm going ta be fine."

"Good, we're getting ready to leave so I'll give you a shout."

"We'll be ready."

"Okay, later," I said and went back to my room grinning widely.

"What's the matter with you?" Penny asked when I entered the room and she saw the expression on my face.

"Blake is going with us."

"In our car?"

"Nope, he's driving Val and following us."

"Did they run off in the night and get married?"

"I think… I hope they didn't. They just spent the night together."

"Oh, I see. So are they ready or still not dressed yet?"

"No, Blake has been busy already, went home and packed then had someone from his precinct drive him back and even called to get time off from work."

"Busy boy, I hope she doesn't break his heart."

"I think he would survive. I just hope they don't break up on the road, or we'll have another passenger."

We had all the luggage out and in the SUV, I saw Blake packing Val's car and he waved. Val finally came out of her room, she looked happy. Penny came up behind me and Val came over.

"Is this serious or just a fling?" Penny asked.

"I'm not sure. Blake does something to me, like no man has before. He may be a few years younger but he's special."

"I thought he had a girlfriend?" I asked.

"He did, but they broke up last month. He just said he had a girlfriend to us at the hospital because I was being too forward with him. I scared him at first."

"Yes Val, you are scary," Penny said.

"Well, he's over being afraid of me," she said.

"Poor guy," I said.

149

Sunshine State Murders

"Thank you, I love you too," Val laughed.

We all got into our cars and after stopping at the motel office to give up our rooms, we headed out towards Orlando on route 17 South. It was a bright sunny day and the humidity was low so far. It was morning yet and we decided to forgo breakfast and pick up lunch just outside Orlando. Blake was keeping up and I was taking my time driving. He was following me carefully, but what I didn't see was someone else carefully following Blake.

We drove straight through until we came up to Orlando city limit and then found a restaurant nearby. We parked and went in, Penny and Val headed right to the restrooms. Blake stood thinking, I said, "Maybe we should use the restroom also."

He nodded and we went to find the men's room. "Are you still okay with driving Val? No problems?"

"No, we had a real nice drive talking about her and everything about her life. Ah think ah know her whole history now," he said with a smirk.

"Did she ask you about your life?"

"We'll discuss that on the return trip. Ah think."

"Are you making long term plans for your life with her?"

"Too early, she said this trip will determine if'n we can get along."

"I want to know what your long term plans are, not hers."

"Ah like her a lot. When we were in the hospital and ah was guarding her, she would talk to me. She is really a nice person and ah like her enough to see where it leads."

"I wish the best for you, just remember she is coming off a bad relationship. She is fragile and maybe just wanting companionship."

"Ah figured that too, so ah'm being cautious."

We left the restroom and found the women sitting at a table already. We sat and examined the menu. The waitress came up and she was a bubbly teenager.

"Good morning or afternoon, it's too close to tell," she smiled and, "I'm Tammy, I'll be your waitress, do you need more time?"

I looked to everyone, they nodded, "Yes, just a couple minutes more, thank you."

"Sure, I'll be back." She went off and I looked to the menu again.

About an hour later we had food and were eating. "I need to find the bookstore for my signing. I'll see if I can find a map of the city."

Val said, "They usually have them at the checkout for the tourists."

"Right, that makes sense." I stood and went to the checkout and there were maps. I bought one city map and took it back to the table. Unfolded it and looked up the street the store was on. I found it.

I pinpointed where we were, followed the roads to the bookstore and then folded the map again.

"Val, have you ever been to Disney World?" I asked.

"When I was a child, my parents brought me here. It was a good memory."

Blake smiled and said, "Ah come here every year with ma family. My nephews love it here."

"Good Blake, you can be our tour guide."

"More than happy to," he said.

"Now we need to find a motel," I said.

"One with a pool," Penny added.

"Yes, one with a pool."

Tammy came bouncing back up with the check and I asked her if she knew where there was a nice motel with a pool.

"I sure do, there's one just off Interstate 4, on Sand Lake Road by the Ripley Museum. I'll get you a brochure from the counter." She went off and came back with a colorful brochure from the motel. It had pictures of a huge pool, which made Penny happy. I could never figure out her fascination for pools and water. I'd have to get her in for analysis on that.

"Okay, it looks good to me." I stood followed by the others and went to pay the check. Blake offered to help, I said he could leave the tip. He went back and I saw him put a couple of bills on the table.

We were back in the cars and heading down Interstate 4 and found the exit to Sand Lake Road. A few minutes later we were in the parking lot and I went with Blake to the office.

We came back with keys and drove around the building until we found our rooms. We parked and went in, Blake came back out and got their luggage, I got ours.

I was out by the car when my cell phone rang and I saw it was Morty. "Hey Morty, we're in Orlando, just arrived."

"Good, I talked to By the Castle Bookstore, where you are going to appear and they have been publicizing since the other day. They are happy that you are going to be there."

"Well, with the delay I hope people will come."

153

Sunshine State Murders

"Hey, it's a gig. I'll send you an email with your updated travel itinerary for the rest of the tour in a few minutes. I'll talk to you tomorrow." He disconnected and I closed up the car.

"Are you going for a swim?" I asked Penny when I came back into the room and saw her in one of her many swimsuits.

"Not so soon after eating, I'm going to rest by the pool and get some sun," she replied.

"Haven't you had enough sun since we hit Florida?"

"Yes, but in moderation, that way you don't burn, and I have plenty of sun block. So where are we going after here?"

"You mean after Orlando? I'm not sure, Morty is sending me a list of places, if we don't get stuck in a murder here."

"Don't even joke about it. If you want me and Willy, we will be by the pool. I'm going to see if Val wants to join us."

"If she and Blake aren't fooling around," I added.

Penny ignored my comment and went out with Willy on his leash. I opened my laptop case and pulled it out, booting the thing up and placing it on the desk in the room. While I waited I looked around the room. It was nice and comfortable, which it should be for the cost. But we were just a stones throw away from Disney World so the rates would be higher. My laptop finished it's opening and I downloaded my email, Morty had sent the tour list. I studied it and then pulled out the travel printer I bought just before we started the trip. I printed out the list and sat back reading.

I looked out the window and could see Penny, Val and Blake all lounging by the pool. They looked very comfortable in the heat and humidity. I was happy in the air-conditioned room. I went online and checked the places where Morty had me going to and the route changed from Washington to Jacksonville then to Savanna, Georgia. After that we were to go to Charleston, South Carolina then up to Raleigh, North Carolina. I guess the plane ride to Washington was out.

My cell phone buzzed and I saw it was Maybell. I hoped we didn't have to go back right away. I answered, "Hey chief, what's up."

"My blood pressure," he said, then, "Got some bad news, we found Steve Myerson this mornin', dead in his motel."

*

Chapter 21

"He was murdered?" I asked.

"Well, were not rightly sure. It looks like a suicide, he was hanging from a ceiling fixture and looks like he kicked out the chair he stood on. Doc is checking him closely, but we don't have the forensic resources to really give him a goin' over. Looks ta me as if he had a guilty conscience and did his self in. How's your trip progressing?"

"We're in Orlando, till the day after tomorrow then up to Jacksonville. Do you need us to swing by?"

"No, just keep on with your trip. Not much you kin do here now. Still haven't found Bonnie, but with this, maybe she's in the clear. Time will tell."

"Sure, keep me informed." We finished and I went to the door and out to the pool. I went to Penny, Val and Blake and sat facing them.

"I have some bad news, depending on how you feel." I was looking right at Val. "Maybell just called me and said they found Steve, dead in his motel room. He hung himself; they say it looks like suicide so far."

Val sat up straight and just stared at me. "Steve would never hang himself. He was stronger than that."

"Well, you didn't know he would beat you either."

She took that in, "I suppose you never know what someone will do." She started tearing up; Blake asked if she wanted to go into the room to rest. She looked to him, took his hand and stood. They quietly went to their room.

"So do you think this is Steve's way of saying he's sorry for attacking Val. That he's guilty of the stabbing?"

"No, I don't. Val was attacked, yes and Steve admits he struck her, but denies stabbing her. I sort of believe him. Now if he only hit her, that's no reason to kill one's self. He would have gotten a light jail sentence but not long enough to stress over it and hang himself. Okay if he did stab her, it would be attempted murder, he may have done it. I really don't know now. But I'm not sure if he was murdered either, the results aren't conclusive enough yet."

"If he was hung, Bonnie couldn't have put him up there," Val said.

"True, Steve was a big guy, it would have taken a stronger person to hoist him up."

"What about Bonnie now, she still on the radar?"

"Well, we assumed she did the stabbing from what Steve told us, but he could have been lying to cover his guilt. Bonnie had a good reason to run if Steve was after her. I'm really confused now."

"That's just old age. Your brain cells are rebelling against all the thinking you do."

157

Sunshine State Murders

"Thanks, I really need to be reminded. Maybell said we didn't need to come back into Palatka. Blake will have to go back there to see if he's going to stay alone, go with Val or they both stay in Palatka. Val can do her edits from anywhere in the world, which is nice. I hope they are careful about their relationship."

"Young love rears it's ugly head. I hope Val isn't too broke up over Steve."

"She has Blake to cry on now. It's good he's here, I wouldn't be a good shoulder for her, I get too emotional."

"Big baby that you are. You are still a good shoulder, even if you have a gooey center. I'm sure you would have been there for her."

"Either way, Blake will help her."

Penny stood, went to the edge of the pool and dove in. I was a bit surprised that she just went in without saying anything. Maybe her gooey center was starting to show too. I went back to the room taking Willy with me, he didn't need to be wet. I sat at my laptop and just stared at it, thinking about the whole mess. Penny was right, the brain cells were not cooperating. I was wearing down now so I went to the bed and plopped down. I picked up Willy and put him on the bed next to me and he plopped down also. We took a quick nap.

I was having a nice dream of standing at the top of a mountain looking out over the Las Vegas valley, with the city all busy and shiny, then I heard a voice telling me to wake up. I opened my eyes and there was Penny standing by the bed watching me.

"Is it time to go home yet?" I asked.

"No, you still have a couple weeks to go. This is turning into one long month. I'm ready to go home, and I'm tired of motels. I'd like to have a kitchen and a bathroom of my own."

I laid there thinking and was hit by inspiration. I got up and found the telephone book in the desk and went through the business pages, I found what I was looking for. I wrote down the address and looked it up on my map and found the area, it was close. Penny had dried off outside earlier and was now putting clothes on. I grabbed Willy, took Penny's hand and went out. I stopped by Val's room and knocked. Blake came to the door and said Val was sleeping. I said that was all right, we were going somewhere and would be back in a while.

In the car we drove to the RV dealer I had found in the telephone book. We pulled in and Penny gave me a look.

"I remember back when we first met, you said that you always wanted a Class B motorhome van, is this what you're up to?"

"They have a great small motorhome that looks like a van, but it is specially designed to be as comfy and convenient as a full size motorhome." I pulled up to the sales office, looked to my left and saw it. A RoadTrek motorhome van, silver and sleek. I got out and took Penny to it, opened the door and we went in. Penny was amazed by the size, layout and standing headroom, just like a small home, complete with kitchen, bath and shower and a bedroom with a really nice queen size bed.

I felt the van shift as the salesman came in. "Howdy folks, looking to buy a motorhome?"

"Found it, can you set up the plates and registration for out of state buyers?"

"We can, you just need insurance and I can do the rest," he said with a big toothy smile at an impending sale.

"This is a used RoadTrek, so it must be at a good price, right?" I asked.

"Yep, fourteen thousand and you can drive it off the lot."

I looked at Penny, she smiled and said, "It's your dream, go for it. I like this better than motels already."

I shook the guy's hand and an hour later after calling my insurance man, I was driving the thing off the lot followed by Penny in the SUV. We arrived back at the motel and I didn't see Val or Blake, so I got the phone book for the location of the car rental place who owned the SUV and told Penny to follow me. We returned the car and drove back to the motel in the van. I was just pulling up to our room when Val and Blake were coming out. Val gave us a stare when she saw Penny and came over. We gave them the nickel tour of the thing and they were impressed.

"What about your room here?" Val asked.

"Oh we'll still keep it and use it, but after we leave here, this is our home away from home."

"Do Blake and I sleep in our car?"

"No, of course not, this thing sleeps six, so four will be just right. We will still get motels for occasional privacy, but this will make the long drive up the coast easier and also back across the United States when we go home to Vegas. Since it looks like a van from the outside, we can park overnight in every Wally World we find."

Val and Blake gave me a blank stare; Penny laughed and said, "Wal-Marts, they don't object to RV's parked overnight in their parking lots. Smart, because travelers need supplies and spend money."

"You two are crazy," Val said and took Blake out of the van.

Penny and I just laughed and she gave me a hug. "Welcome home Sweetie."

I looked to the back bedroom and said, "Shall we christen it?"

"Maybe later, I think Val and Blake are waiting for us," she said and went out.

"Darn, later then," I said to the van and followed her.

Sunshine State Murders

We were hungry now and it was around dinnertime so we walked to a restaurant across the street and had dinner. We had a good southern meal and we sat talking. "How are you feeling now Val?" Penny asked.

"I'm better, now that I took a nap. I'm really sorry for Steve, he was a decent person when he wasn't being a monster. I'll get over it." She looked to Blake and smiled. We talked a bit longer and I nearly bored them with stories about the van and what it could do, then we went back to the motel.

I had everyone pile into the van and drove over to the bookstore to take a look. Val and Blake were both impressed with the van now that they spent some time in it.

"It's a cute little home, isn't it?" Penny said.

"I've never been one to sleep outdoors, unless I'm drunk and passed out in a parking lot," Val said with a huge laugh.

*

Chapter 22

We arrived at the bookstore and I was so happy that the van parked well into one of the small spaces out front.

I looked around and asked Penny where Willy was. "I thought you had him," she said.

I stood and called him, then I heard a tiny yip in the back, I went there and found the dog lying on the bed. I wondered how he got up there, then he went to the side of the bed where there was a box that he jumped down to, and came around to me. I picked him up and petted him saying how good he was. I called to Penny saying I found him, I guess I had brought him and then set him down when I got into the van. He found his way to the bedroom.

We exited the van and went to the front door of the store; it was a fairly big building and full of books. Good to see that paper books still were in demand. Electronic books were starting to pass book sales over paper; it was a worry for publishers.

We wandered the store first to get a feel for it and then I went to the counter and asked for Barry Simpson. The girl behind the counter yelled for Barry, who was shelving books and popped out to see what was going on.

He came forward and asked, "Can I help you?"

I was a little hurt that he didn't recognize me, but figured he had a lot of books so he probably missed seeing my photo on the book jacket.

"Ah! You are Jim Richards, I recognize you now from your stand-up," he said and pointed behind me.

I turned and I was looking at me looking back at me. It was a life-size cardboard stand-up with my photo looking debonair, holding my books. I went to it and admired the image. I remembered when they took the photos. Penny came up behind me and laughed.

"I want this, I have to have this." She turned to Barry and said, "Can I have this when my husband's book signing is over?"

"For you Mrs. Wickens-Richards, anything. I really miss seeing you on TV. I'll have it packed in the box right after the signing and you can take it."

"What are you going to do with this?" I asked.

"Probably have more fun than I do with you." She laughed and went back to our friends. I just stood watching her go. I looked back to the photo and gave me a shot with my finger, "Nice," I said.

Barry was all excited about my being there and gave us a tour of the place. It was large and had more books than I saw in most the bookstores I had been in.

"We get a huge amount of people here on vacation, who need something to read while sitting around the motels. The locals all are tired of the vacationers so they stay home and read. Either way it's win-win for me," he said with a grin. "You are scheduled to be here tomorrow at five and I know a dozen people who are looking forward to it."

I hoped there would be more than a dozen people. "Barry, I'll be here on time, so don't worry."

He asked us a few more polite questions then said he had to get my display set up now that he knew I was in town and went off. I looked back to me and smiled. Penny said, "Get over yourself." Then she went to the front door and out.

We headed back to the motel and parked. Val and Blake said they were going to the room to relax. I knew that was code for fooling around, sex even. Penny and I sat in the van a bit longer.

"I want to stay the night in here," Penny said. I smiled and said that was good with me. I was glad she was liking the van.

I looked back and said we need some sheets for the bed and a few supplies, so we could go to a WalMart I saw down the road we were on. We went there, I put Willy in his travel bag and we went in. About an hour later, we came out with two carts of goodies for the van. We piled everything in and drove back to the motel. I parked away from our room so not to be disturbed and we put everything in place. The RV center had prepared the van for us, putting propane in the tanks and filling the water supply. There was a generator for charging the battery supply for the internal electricity, so we were prepared for the night.

Sunshine State Murders

Penny fixed a snack with food we bought and put in the fridge. We set up the bedroom with the new sheets and spread out on the big comfy mattress. I had turned the built in TV around so we could see it and we had our snacks and beer I bought and watched TV. Willy was relaxing at the end of the bed.

I looked to Penny and said, "Just like home." Later we christened the van, it was good.

The next morning I woke feeling really refreshed and went to the bathroom and did my business. Then Penny took over, and I sat in the captain's chair up front after I took down the curtains covering the front windows.

As I sat there, my cell phone buzzed and I saw it was Maybell. "Good morning. What's up now."

"Ah had forensic people from Gainesville come in ta examine the body of Myerson. Final result was that he was murdered."

I felt a chill and asked how they knew.

"They found fresh abrasions on his wrists showing that he was tied while he hung. They say the bindings were removed after he was dead. Now the man couldn't have hung his self if'n he was tied up now could he?"

"No and Penny asked me if Bonnie could have killed him when we theorized what may have happened, but Bonnie was too small to lift him up there."

Bob Moats

"Got that right, now we got us a mystery. You're the big city P.I., y'all come up with an answer."

"Well, I'll see what I can deduce. My book signing here is tonight, we can swing by tomorrow on the way back up to Jacksonville. My book signing there isn't for a few days."

He said that would be good and hung up. Now I was concerned. Penny wouldn't like to find out Steve was murdered, and the killer is still out there.

Penny came out of the bathroom, all clean and happy. She said to set up the table she saw in the literature on the van. I pulled the parts out, set them up and swiveled the captain's chairs around to face the table. Penny went to the fridge, got out some eggs and bacon and pulled the skillet we bought in a cooking set. She used the kitchen to make breakfast and we ate. It was actually good.

As I was munching on a piece of bacon I said, "I got a call from Maybell while you were in the bathroom, he said that a forensic team from Gainesville check the body of Steve and…"

"He was murdered wasn't he?" Penny finished my sentence.

"Yep, that's the final opinion. Maybell isn't happy. I said we could swing by on the way to Jacksonville. I'll tell Val and Blake, he may want to stay in Palatka to help with any investigation."

Sunshine State Murders

"That damn curse of yours," she said and then said no more.

We finished the meal and I did the dishes, just as there was a knock on the door. I went to see Val standing there.

"I went to your room and pounded but you didn't answer, then I saw the van was not parked in front so I searched and found you hiding back here. Is this going to be regular thing?"

I laughed and invited her in, "No, we just wanted to try it out. It was very nice."

She sniffed and said, "Do I smell bacon?"

Penny smiled and asked if she wanted some, Val sat at the table and said, "I hope the table service is good here."

I pulled my cell phone and called Blake, telling him to find us for breakfast. A few minutes later he showed up and Penny and I served them breakfast.

We were all sitting around the table after they finished and I said, "Got word from Maybell a while ago that they examined Steve's body and the result is… he was murdered."

Val took that harder than hearing he committed suicide. "Who is doing all this? Stabbing me, and now killing Steve. This is not good."

"I have my book signing tonight, then tomorrow morning we will stop back in Palatka on the way north to see what we can do. Is that all right with you?" I asked Val and Blake.

Blake spoke first, "This is goin' to be a major case, so ah probably will be needed." He looked to Val; she just sat there.

"I guess we have to go. I should give them names of his relatives so they can claim his body." She turned to Blake, "You have to work, so I'll accept that." She and Blake went out after thanking us for the breakfast. I looked to Penny who was quiet.

I said, "I'm thinking Val regrets coming here now."

*

Chapter 23

I pulled the van back to the parking in front of our room and we went in. Penny went straight for the pool after changing. I sat by the poolside and wondered how Val was holding up. This was a stressful week for her. Penny swam up to the edge of the pool and smiled to me.

"The only thing I will miss with traveling in the van is a lack of a pool," she said.

"We can always go to a beach. If you can go swim

into a lake or ocean. Or I'll haul a trailer filled with water for you."

"I guess I'll have to get used to it. Are we going to drive all the way across country in the van?"

"It looks that way, it's all we have now to get back home."

"Good, I like the van," she said and swam off.

I was happy that she accepted the van so easily. I sat watching her and Willy swim around enjoying themselves, then I went into the room to get online to check my email. I had a couple emails from Lacey asking when we were coming home. Earl, Trapper and Buck were getting under her skin. I had to smile at that. I'm glad she depends on me to protect her from my evil partners.

I sent a message back telling her about the van and saying we'd be back in a couple weeks. I sent the email and as I was sitting there, a message came back to me. I read it and she said to come back quickly. They were in the process of moving the business and I really needed to be there to get a good office. I replied to claim a good one for me and protect it with her life. I sent it. She replied she would and to get back soon.

I closed up my computer and sat looking out the window. Penny was now out of the pool and drying off. She was so beautiful, I was so lucky to have her.

I stood and went out, she was coming towards me and I grabbed on to her with a big hug and a sloppy kiss.

She pulled back and said, "What got into you?"

"You did," I said. "Lacey said they are moving the office to bigger quarters. Earl already told me but they are now doing it. I hope they tell me where it's at so I can find it."

She patted my shoulder and said, "Maybe it's better that you don't find the new building." She went to the room and I followed.

We spent the day just resting until about four, when we got ready for the signing. Val and Blake were ready to go and we all piled into the van and drove back to the bookstore. We entered the store and there were people lining up to meet me, I was happy. We had a good night with the signing and the evening ended. I drove everyone back and said that we should leave early in the morning to return to Palatka. Val and Blake agreed and went to their room. Penny and I decided to stay in the motel room since we paid for it and relaxed the night with beer, chips and TV.

Next morning, we put all our baggage into the van as Blake did with theirs in Val's car. We checked out of the motel and drove out of Orlando, we didn't even get to see Disney world. Oh well, one other day. Murder waits for no one. Besides my book tour really didn't give much time for sightseeing.

We drove back up northward and arrived back in Palatka in about two hours of casual driving. We went straight to the Palatka police precinct and parked. Blake got out of Val's car and said he was going to check in with his department to see if they needed him, he went off. Val stuck close to us; I think she was nervous that there was a killer still out there.

I was going to go in to find Maybell, the women decided to stay in the van to relax. I told Penny to have her .38 handy, she said she would.

"Y'all solved the case yet?" he said when he saw me in the hallway outside his office.

"I wish," I said and came into the room. "I did some thinking on the way up. Ken Parker was someone I had thought about in the attack of Val. He was shot down when he hit on Val, and maybe he had something against her for it. Could he have strung up Steve."

"Ken is someone ah have had on ma list, but he's crippled, had his leg crushed in a car accident. So ah'm not sure if he could have taken on Steve and subdued him to hang."

I thought on that, "So who else would have motive to kill Steve?"

"Well y'all have ta come up with somethin', I'm out of ideas ma'self"

"I'll think on it, now what were the circumstances around his death?"

"I had a man on him after y'all left, jest to watch, but he never came out of his room. Ma officer went to the window and could see him hanging, he called us in."

"Did the doc say when he died?"

"Yep, the other night jest before you and your friends left to Orlando in the morning. Was Val with y'all the whole time after Steve came to your room?"

"She never left us or Blake. Oh, you do know that Blake is involved with Val now?"

"The boy is foolish, but he'll come to his senses soon."

"I just hope he doesn't get hurt," I said.

"We kin have one of them interventions if'n he gets in too deep," Maybell said with a grin.

We talked about the trip to Orlando and I told him about the van. His eyes lit up and asked if he could see it, so I took him out and showed it to him,

"Ah always wanted one of these, maybe when ah retire."

I found the note saying Penny and Val had taken Willy for a walk around the block. Maybell was exploring the van when Blake came back.

"They said they don't need me, so ah'm back. Where's Val?"

"She and Penny took a walk around the block.

Sunshine State Murders

Maybell is in here checking the van out."

Maybell came up behind me, "Hey boy, y'all got your head up your ass? Y'all crazy to get involved with women. What about that girl, Betty, you used ta date?"

"We broke up last month. Ah like Val now and Ah'm not gettin' in deep until ah know what she wants."

"Run, boy, run fast and far," Maybell said and got out of the van then turned to me, "Mighty nice rig, ah'll have ta consider one someday." He gave Blake a fatherly whack on the head and went back to the precinct.

Blake and I stood by the van watching for the women. I suddenly saw Penny holding Willy as they came running around a hedge at the end of the block; she was alone. We went to her and I yelled "Where's Val?"

I could see panic on her face, "She's gone!"

She got to us and I asked "Where?"

"How the hell should I know. We got to a small party store and I said I wanted a Pepsi, she said she was going to stay outside in the fresh air. I went in and when I came out, she was gone. Damn, I shouldn't have left her alone!"

"Okay, Blake go back in and start a search, I'll tell Maybell." We all went into the building and Blake went to the desk sergeant, Penny and I went to Maybell's office.

I came around the door opening and said to him,

Bob Moats

"Someone grabbed Val! She's gone!"

"Hell you say," He said and got on his phone calling for his men to get to his office. A couple minutes later five detectives assembled in the room as Penny explained what happened. Maybell told his men to go back to the party store and start a sweep, question everyone. He gave a description of Val and told them to move. They all took off and I said to Penny, "Let's go there and see what we can find out."

Blake came running to us in the hall and said he was riding with a patrol car and would keep us informed by cell phone. I told him where we were going and we split up.

I drove the van out using Penny's directions and we came to the party store. I saw a few officers talking to people in the area and then we parked and got out.

Penny had described what happened and went through it pointing out the scene. One of Maybell's detectives was standing by us listening and asked Penny if she remembered any cars or trucks in the parking lot.

"I wasn't really paying much attention to the parking lot. We were gabbing about things and then I went in. I wasn't gone for more than three or four minutes, I found the pop can and paid, then came right back out. She wasn't here. I yelled for her thinking she may have gone around the building but I realized she was not here."

"You carried Willy in with you?" I asked.

"Yes, I picked him up and took him with me. Damn, I should never have left her alone."

Blake pulled up in a patrol car and came to us. He looked stressed, "We got to find her Jim, who would have done this?"

*

Chapter 24

I saw Penny was on the verge of tears, I took her to the van and told her to relax. "I need to do something," she protested.

"There's nothing you can do right now, let the cops deal with it. I'm going to do what I can, I'll get Blake to work with me. You just stay safe and keep that gun handy, you hear?"

She looked so sad to me, I kissed her cheek and said to relax and lock the doors. I got out and heard her hit the door lock button. I went to Blake, he looked just as bad as Penny.

"What shall we do?" I asked.

"We asked everyone in the area, no one saw anything. This is amazing, all these people and no one is saying anything. I'm pissed."

"Okay, are there any security cameras in the area?" I was always used to the myriad of cameras around Vegas, they helped so much in my investigations there.

He looked around, saw nothing. "Let's check in the store to see if'n they have cameras inside," he said.

We went in and Blake went to the man behind the counter. Blake flashed his badge and asked, "Sir, do y'all have security cameras on the premises?"

The man pointed to one over the cash register, it was pointed outwards and could possibly see the parking lot. I asked, "As you now know there was a possible kidnapping out front and your camera may have picked up the incident, can we see the tapes?"

He called some other man in the store who came over. "Hector, take these officers to the back and show them the security recorder. Help them to see what they need."

I thanked him and we followed Hector back. We went into what amounted to a storeroom and then to a small room in the back of that. We entered and he pointed to a desk and shelves with a recorder and monitor on it. He went to it and asked how far back?

"About an hour to start, I'll tell you when to go forward or stop, thanks," I said.

He fiddled with the recorder and the monitor lit with a picture of the store checkout counter, I could see the parking lot in the background, but there was not much coverage. We watched for a few minutes then we could see Val and Penny coming from the sidewalk to the front of the store. I ask Hector to be ready to stop and pointed to the women.

We could see them talking and then Penny picked up Willy and went to the door. Val stood back and was looking around. Penny walked past the counter and then we could see that Val looked to her left and said something to someone off camera. She went that way and then we saw Penny come back with her Pepsi, paying for it and went back to the entrance. I watched for any vehicle driving out, then I saw a light colored van drive across the front just as Penny went out. We could see her standing, looking around and then got panicky and ran around the front, out of sight of the camera, then we saw her run back to the sidewalk heading back to where we were.

"Hector, take this tape out and give it to Officer Shelby here. Blake, take it back to Maybell and see what he says and if they can get the van's plates off it." He agreed as Hector pulled the tape out and replaced it with another. Blake took the tape and we left.

I got back to the van as Penny unlocked the doors for me. I slid in the driver's seat and sat. "We have a tape that shows you and Val, but it doesn't show how she was taken. It looks like she was talking to someone, then went off the security camera coverage. We only saw one van drive away but it could have been anyone's van. Hopefully they can get the plate's number off the video and find the owner."

She sat there quietly. "I know how it feels to be

kidnapped, more than once. The fear and terror going through my head, not knowing if I would see you again or if I was going to live. It was the longest time I spent not knowing what was going to happen. It's different when things happen fast, like my shooting Nick North when he threatened to shoot you. That was quick and you can't stop to think. But get kidnapped, that is so long and painful having to wonder when I was going to die. I can understand what Val is going through. Jim, please find her."

"I'll do my best, besides Morty will be pissed if I don't find her."

She smiled, "Funny, but not. Just find her."

"I will," I said quietly.

We were back at the precinct, in the detective's bullpen. Everyone was on phones and studying the crime board they set up with information they were now getting.

Blake came up and said, "A few of the detectives beat the bushes and found a couple witnesses who said they saw a blond woman talkin' ta someone in a light colored van, but they didn't pay enough attention to see if she got in the van or was pulled in. The tape is being looked over to get the plates off it. Ah hope that we can get an ID. Our resources here are limited, but they are doing their best to enhance the tape."

He pulled Penny and me aside and said, "Jim, we need to find her, ah'm getting really attached to her. Ah'll do anything to git her back, help me please."

Sunshine State Murders

"Blake, I'll do what I can. All we can do now is wait on the plates and hope some other witness comes forward. I heard Maybell say they were putting the kidnapping on the TV and radio, maybe it will help. Now why would someone take her? She isn't rich or famous, think, what would be the reason?"

Blake looked blank, "Ah don't have any idea, like y'all said she wasn't anyone special, other than to me." He paused, "Let's sit and go over everything since y'all and she got here."

I said that was a good idea. The three of us went to a desk off the side and sat. I went over our trip here and our meeting Val the first time. We covered the book signing, Bonnie's threat and the bar that Blake took us to.

"Now Ken Parker tried to hit on Val, but she shot him down, do you think that he could be the cause for all this?" I said.

"As I said before Ken is an odd duck but ah don't think he'd do this. He's crippled and not very strong, he's old. Sorry, I'm not saying old people can't be bad people. Ah'm sure you are a good person despite your advanced age."

"Okay, Blake stop before you say something worse." I smiled to relieve his tension.

"Sorry, now why would he be so incensed to kidnap Val or to kill Myerson?"

"I'm wondering if Myerson may have interrupted Val being stabbed, and the killer wanted Myerson out of the picture. How's that sound?"

"Make sense, did Myerson say he saw anything else besides Bonnie being there?"

"No, but he may have missed what really happened. He came back to see if Val was all right and said he saw Bonnie standing in the bushes, but I don't think she could have kidnapped Val today. Val would never have gone near Bonnie. I think we need to go visit Parker at the bookstore, it's something we can do at least."

Blake agreed and we went out to the van. I drove back to the bookstore using Blake's directions. I pulled in a parking space up front and we went in. The place was quiet and there was one girl at the counter. I went to her and asked, "Hi, is Ken in?"

She smiled and said, "No, he's taking a few days off to relax. I think I heard him say he was going to his cabin again over near the Ocala National Forest around some town called Fruitland. Funny name huh? He goes there every couple months."

"Does Ken drive a van?" I asked.

"No, he has a Nissan, but he uses a friend's van occasionally when he has to deliver books."

"Do you know what kind of van?"

"Sure, he brings it here to load up, I get to see it. It's a Chevy 250, light brown in color."

I was now sure Ken had something to do with this. "Do you have any way of telling us how to find his cabin? It's important we find him."

She went to a card file and looked through it, then wrote down an address, handing it to me.

"Thanks, this will help." We went back to the van and I pulled my cell phone and called Maybell. I explained what we had deduced and gave him the address the girl gave us. He thanked me and said he'd get someone on it.

I put the phone away and sat. "Blake, have there been any other women disappearing from town in the last year or so?"

"Sure, every so often some woman goes off and vanishes. Why?"

"I'm wondering if these disappearances coincide with Ken's trip to his cabin."

"Ah kin find out. We'd need to know when Ken goes to his cabin."

"The girl said every couple of months, see how often the women disappeared."

Blake pulled his phone and called someone, a few minutes later he got a call back and he was listening. He asked if I had a pen and paper, I said I did and gave him what he needed. He finished and handed me the paper.

I looked at it, "Every couple months there were women who disappeared. I think we may have a serial killer."

*

Chapter 25

We were now thinking about Val in the clutches of Ken, if he was a serial killer. I looked to Blake and Penny and said, "Shall we go to the cabin?"

They both spoke at the same time with an resounding 'yes'. I said, "Then sit back and Blake guide me there." I asked him where I needed to go and he directed me out.

We were heading down the 309 and went through Nashua, as Blake was getting anxious. I smiled and said, "Blake don't get your hopes up, we could be wrong. This could be a waste of time, but it's something and I feel it's worth our time. But let's go into this with a clear head. Agreed?"

He stared ahead and quietly said, "Agreed."

We drove on and I was just entering Fruitland and then asked Blake to tell me where to go.

"I don't know, I've never been in Fruitland, just

passed through it. We can stop and ask."

"Sure, it's the right thing to do." I pulled into a service station and got out. Blake followed me, I told Penny to wait. We went in and asked the attendant at the counter if he knew where the cabin would be for the address we had. He looked at it and did some slow thinking, I gave him the time but Blake was getting impatient.

He pulled his badge and said, "If you can hurry up and give us the information, this is a matter of life and death."

The man was now thinking harder and told us where to go. It was just into the wilderness he said. The cabin was owned by a nice man who came by to get gas often.

"You know this man?" I asked.

"Just to talk while pumping gas for him. He has told me about his cabin and he comes down here every so often. Very talkative man."

"Does he come out with a van or a car?" Blake asked.

"Oh, he always has a van, a tan one. He had trouble one time he came out and I had to put a new belt in the engine."

"Have you ever seen inside the van?"

"Had to, the engine is partly accessed from the inside of the cab."

"Did you notice anything strange inside the van?"

"Nope, it was usually empty. A few burlap bags and some ropes but nothing else."

"Has he passed through here lately?" I asked.

"Sure, he stopped about an hour ago, and got gas before going out into the forest."

I looked to Blake and thanked the man. We went out to the van and sat. I called Maybell and told him where we were.

He said, "Ah got men on the way out there, they just left. Ah did some checking from your report and the women who vanished were all blond. Ah'd say it is a good bet he's into this up to his neck. Be careful and tell Blake not to get shot."

"I'll tell him, we will watch our selves. But time is short and Val may even be dead all ready. So if your men aren't here soon, we go in." I hung up; I didn't want him telling me not to do anything foolish. I could deny his responsibility if we got killed.

I pulled out and down the road towards where the gas jockey told us to go. We took a while going down the dirt road that branched off the main road. I didn't want to bust something on the van on the rutted road. We watched for the cabin or the van but saw nothing.

"I hope that man gave us the right directions. This is going way into the woods, I'm not even sure if I can turn around now. The road is too narrow."

"I'm sure we can find a clearing to turn, but we need to find them," Blake said.

"I'm not even sure how far into this we have to go. The man didn't say."

We drove on and then I could see a cabin ahead. Blake saw it and got excited. We drove on and finally got close. I stopped away from the cabin so as not to alert Parker that we were there. I told Penny that she had to stay in the van, and to lock the doors. She protested but I was firm.

"I want to help Val," she said.

"I understand, but wait here and watch us. If you see anything wrong, call me."

"All right, but keep in touch with me too."

"I will, just keep your .38 handy." I leaned back and kissed her, and then Blake and I went out.

We went cautiously towards the cabin. I couldn't see a van anywhere near the wooden structure. I hoped we hadn't missed him, or got there before him. Blake was following me, we both had our weapons out and ready. We were about fifty feet from the cabin, I pointed to a path that looked like it led to the back of the building. We went that way and finally came out to the back of the place.

I saw a hole dug into the ground, the dirt piled up next to it. I pointed it out to Blake and he said that there was fresh dirt mounded a couple places around the yard. I could see them, they looked like graves. I got a chill thinking what we would find. We carefully went through the yard and came up to the back door.

I cautiously looked through a window in back and didn't see anyone inside. Blake went around to one side of the building as I went to the other. I told him to be careful. I was checking all the windows but still saw nothing. I went to a window in front and looked in. I still saw nothing and there was no van anywhere around the building.

I came around and was startled by Blake coming the other way. "I don't see anything," he said quietly.

"Yeah, either they aren't here or they are hidden inside. Let's take a look inside."

"Should we wait for a warrant?" he asked.

"Blake you are a cop, you need a warrant, but I don't. So just follow me."

We went to the front door and I pounded on it, yelling, "Ken Parker, open up it's Jim Richards."

Nothing, so I pounded again. Nothing. "Screw it," I

187

said and brought my foot up and pushed forward into the door, it gave way.

We went in with guns out front and checked the place; it was empty. "Damn, the gas station attendant said he was an hour ahead of us. Where could he be?"

We searched the rooms and I opened one door and was shocked. I called Blake and he came up behind me. The room was empty of furniture other than mattresses on the floor. There were chains affixed to the walls and hand cuffs on the loose ends. "Looks like he kept women here, chained to the walls." I saw what looked like blood on one of the three mattresses and told Blake to call Maybell and tell him what we found.

He was talking to Maybell when my cell phone rang; it was Penny. "Are you okay?" I asked.

"I'm fine, just wanted to know if you two were all right. Did you find Val?"

"Not yet, we're still looking, but we found where Parker may have kept women captive. I'll tell you more about it later, just be patient."

"Okay, be careful," she said and hung up.

Blake came to me and said, "Maybell said to shoot first and ask questions later, but ah don't think he meant it. He said his men are still on the way, but don't know where to go, yet. Ah gave him directions and he said he'd pass them along. Is this what ah think it is? He held women here against their will."

188

"Looks that way, let's do a search of the cabin and in the drawers, anywhere we might find evidence."

We dug through the place and I found a locker with women's clothing in it. Articles of personal effects with purses, that still had identifications in them. I called Blake and asked for the list that he carried, we checked the names he wrote from his call to the licenses and they matched.

"We got us a killer. Now if we can find out where he took Val," I said.

We went out back to look at the graves that he had dug. The new one wasn't very deep, the rest were still fresh and hadn't been covered too well. I took a shovel that was leaning on the dirt pile and dug a bit from the one grave that looked the freshest. About a foot down I found a hand sticking out. It was wrinkled and decomposing, but it was human. I stopped, my stomach was turning now and walked away from the grave, Blake just stood looking down and then he vomited.

I was on the verge of it also but held on. I counted nine small mounds of graves in all, including the newly dug one. I presumed it was for Val. But what did he do with the women, did he kill and bury them or just tortured them and then sexually assaulted before he murdered them?

I told Blake to follow me back to the van, we would wait until the other cops got there. We walked up the path to where I had left the van and when we got there, I saw him. Ken was standing next to the van with a gun to Penny's head.

*

Chapter 26

I was shocked to see Penny outside the van with Parker. "You harm her Parker, and you are dead."

"Big threats from the big writer. I still have Val and you won't find her. Now drop your guns and come forward."

We were still too far away for either of us to get a good kill shot. I didn't want to hit Penny if I got stupid and tried to hit Parker. I said quietly to Blake to just follow my lead.

"Come on Richards, drop them."

"Sorry Ken, that only works in the movies, you shoot Penny and you are definitely dead. So you can't kill her."

"How about I shoot her in the leg?"

"Then you'll have to carry her to get away. You don't have a lot of options. Why don't you just give it up?"

"Because I still have Val tucked away, if you don't

find her soon, she'll die. I do read books and have learned to confine my victims with enough air to help me make a clean get-away. Now I have the upper hand, so drop your guns and come forward, now!"

"Tell me Ken what happened that night, did you stab Val?" I was stalling for time, hoping Maybell's cops would show up.

He gave me an evil smile, I hoped he had a big enough head to brag on his accomplishment.

"Sure I'll tell you, I was in the back parking lot near the room where Val was staying. I saw her finally come around the building. I was going to grab her then, but some guy came up to her and they started arguing. She turned and he grabbed a rock and hit her, then the coward took off. I went to her, she was still barely breathing, I decided she was too damaged to take, so I pulled my sword from my cane, yes it is a sword cane, and I stabbed her over and over. Then I heard someone coming and it was the guy who hit her, coming back. I went back to the parking lot and watched him come to her, he was bending down to her when that psycho bitch who stalked you came walking through the bushes by the building. She came out and the man saw her. He went to her and grabbed her arm, but she screamed and pulled away, then ran, he went after her. I was still watching when you, that cop and your wife came running around the building. The rest you know."

Penny tried to pull away but he shook her and pushed the gun harder to her head.

He yelled now, "I thought that guy may have seen me

191

so I found out who he was and looked for him. Luckily I found his motel and after he was set free from jail I went to visit him, you know what happened there."

"I was told you were crippled, how could you have hung Myerson?"

"I'm not as crippled as I let people believe, I'm actually very strong. I find when I need to take my trophies, my women, it's better if people think poor old Ken is too crippled to do anything bad. It's worked well in the past. I got the drop on Stevie boy and strung him up to make it look like he was regretful that he almost killed the woman. I've been following you to see what you were up to, then I saw Val standing outside that party store, I pulled up and Val came over. I had a gun on her and told her to get in the van or I'd kill her and your wife. She obliged me and then I drove away. Once I was away from the store, I tied her up and drove out here. But I didn't come to the cabin yet, I had some running to do, then came here and found your van. Your wife was out letting your dog crap and I snuck up behind her. But you came back too soon. Did you get a good look at my trophies?"

"You're a psycho Parker, you can't get away now that we know, you'll be hunted no matter where you go."

"Oh come on Richards, that's good for fiction, but there are thousands of people like me who are hiding out from the law, I got resources and a lot of cash stashed to let me live comfortably for a long time. Now I need to go, I won't harm your dear wife as long as you stay back and I can leave."

Bob Moats

He started to walk Penny away from the van just as a shot rang out from the woods to our right. Parker screamed and I could see he was hit in the shoulder, too damn close to Penny, but he let up on his hold and she dropped. Blake and I had a better shot now but he turned and ran to the back of the van. From our position, we couldn't see where he went to. I heard another shot, it sounded like rifle fire and then I heard thrashing in the woods to our left. He had gotten away.

I ran to Penny followed by Blake, she said she was all right and to go find Parker and Val.

"Blake, see if you can track him." He said he would and went off. I helped Penny up just as Willy came running out from under the Van. I picked him up, took Penny to the van and got her in.

"Where's your gun?"

"I left it on the seat, stupid thing to do."

"Okay, grab it and go to the rear of the van and lay low until I get back." I closed the door after pushing the door lock button. I yelled through the window, "If Willy has to crap, let him do it in the van."

I turned to the woods and tried to see if I could sight the person who shot at Parker, but the woods were quiet now. I heard a shot from where Blake went so I ran in that direction. I was yelling for Blake when I entered the thick brush and trees. I heard him ahead of me, calling. I ran in the direction of his voice when I heard two more shots. I yelled again for Blake and heard nothing.

193

Sunshine State Murders

I came up to a small clearing and found Blake on the ground. I went to him and he had a head wound, enough to knock him out but he was still breathing. I looked around and then pulled Blake back under some brush to hide him. I stood and listened for noise but heard none. I went in the direction of the only path I saw, then heard noise ahead. I was wondering where Parker had his van, he said he came up behind us. Maybe he doubled back and went to his van. I was starting to worry about Blake and went back.

He was sitting up now and stared at me. "Did you get him?" he asked.

"No, he's gone, are you well enough to go back?"

"Yes, I need to find Val." He stood with my help. The wound on his temple wasn't bad, just enough to stun him. We went back in the direction we came and returned to my van. I yelled for Penny and she came out.

I helped Blake to sit on the ground just as I heard vehicles coming up the road. I turned to see two of Palatka's patrol cars barreling down the dirt road. They pulled up and four men got out, two went to Blake and the others came to me.

"We got here as fast as we could, the directions took us out of the way but we doubled back and found the dirt road. Where's Parker?"

"Either still in the woods or he got back to his van. You didn't see a tan colored van on the way in here?"

194

"Yes, it's back a ways down this road. One of our cars stopped to check it."

"Call them on the radio and tell them to check inside and stay with it, it's Parkers van. He may try to go back to it."

The lead man went to his car and called. I asked if any of them had gotten here earlier and was shooting from the woods.

"No sir, we just now arrived. None of us could have done it."

"I'd recommend that one car go back to the junction of the dirt road by the highway and watch for him coming out."

The men with Blake said they'd take him and go sit where I said. Blake looked to me with a hopeful face.

"Don't worry Blake we'll find her." They went to the car, turned it around in the clearing ahead and went back.

I turned to the lead cop and said, "Parker is in the woods, he knows the area and we don't, so we should go to his cabin and wait to see what happens. You can tie up the crime scene there and call the locals to come out and help."

He told his partner to drive up to the cabin and they left. Penny and I stood next to the van and she grabbed on to me.

"I was so worried he would shoot you."

"He could have knowing I wouldn't have shot at him with you in front. I don't know why he didn't."

"Well he probably wanted to brag for a bit. But who shot at him?"

"I haven't the foggiest idea, but it was a good thing they did." My cell phone buzzed, I saw it was Blake.

"Mr. Richards, Parker just left in a station wagon from another dirt road next to this one. We're following him back north on 309, towards Fruitville. It looks like he has a large box in the back of the wagon, maybe Val is in that?"

"It's possible, just keep on him and call ahead for the local cops to set up a road block and keep me informed." I turned to Penny, "Get in, they're in pursuit now."

*

Chapter 27

I drove down to the cabin and told the police there what was happening and then turned around and went back out the dirt road. I got back on County Road 309 and headed north. I put my Bluetooth earpiece in and used the voice command to dial Blake on my phone.

Bob Moats

I heard the cell phone dialing the number, then Blake came on. "Blake, where are you?"

"We're still on County Road 309, we went through Fruitland and Parker nearly killed a few people running red lights. We're coming up on Fort Gates Ferry Road. He's still moving."

"Okay I'll keep the phone line open so you can fill me in on your progress."

He said that would be fine with him and I listened in as the cops talked about how Parker was nuts by the way he was driving. I told Penny I had Blake on my phone and was listening to their pursuit.

They were quiet for a while as I could hear the siren on the car blaring now. Blake finally yelled that Parker was turning. The other cops were still pointing out his progress, through the radio, I assumed to the local cops. Blake said to me, "He's turned left on Forest Trail Road, there's a sign so you should be able to find it."

I had already passed Fruitland and saw the damage Parker had caused. We drove the few more miles and found Forest Trail Road and turned left. "Where are you now Blake?"

"Turn on the first right, it is still Forest Trail, but it goes up through the forest and all the way back out to 309, but it's a long road."

"I see the turn, we're behind you. I can see the dust you're stirring up."

197

Sunshine State Murders

I kept on the road driving as carefully as the van would let me. I was happy that the people who made the van made it aerodynamically fast.

"He's turned again, but we passed the turn. We're going back so watch for us. He's heading into the Waleka State Forest. If he tries to go on foot he'll end up in the lake of Mud Creek Cove."

"You must really know this area Blake," I said.

"Not really, I'm following on the road atlas," he laughed.

"Sounds good to me."

"Damn Mike, he's pulled into that grove of trees we passed, go back." I heard someone say and then I heard the car sounding like it was driving through a field of brush.

"Jim, he's pulled off and parked, we're coming up on the car now. Crap, the back is opened and the box is out on the ground. It looks like he took Val out and they are on foot."

"I'm coming up to where you are, I see the dust still floating."

"I see you, so be ready to turn."

"I see you also, here we come." I hung up my phone and pulled up behind the patrol car. Penny and I got out and went to where Blake was standing by the station wagon. There was a long wooden box out on the ground and the top was opened. Blake turned to me and said, "He probably had her in this, they are out there now. I called for the sheriffs and they said they'd have a copter in the air shortly to do some spotting."

"You said that there's a lake ahead?"

"Yep, Mud Creek Cove. Unless he has a boat here, he's not going very far."

The second and third patrol cars that came to Parker's cabin came flying up the road and parked. The men got out and the lead cop said they were going to spread out and search. Blake said to be careful and not to shot his captive.

I looked to Penny and said, "We can go stumbling through the woods, and possibly get lost or wait here and let the police do what they are trained for."

She had to agree, "We would do no good out there, it's not like running around the streets of Vegas."

Blake had already ran into the woods and a few minutes later I could hear the copter flying over. I was listening to the patrol car radio blaring out the men reporting their progress. I stood next to Penny as she took my hand.

Sunshine State Murders

"I hope they find Val alive. I was just getting to really like her as a friend."

I put my arm around her and pulled her in, she put her head on my shoulder and I could feel the tension in her. I thought I heard another car and looked down the road but saw nothing. I thought it might be the local police but no car came by.

We stood for what seemed like hours and listened to the radio, no progress was being made. I heard Blake say that it looked like Parker had vanished. They said that they made it to the lake and were going to turn back.

I was leaning on the front of our van when I heard noises from the woods. I turned expecting to see the police but I was surprised to see Parker and Val thrashing out of the brush. Val had duct tape across her mouth and her hands were tied behind her.

Penny had her .38 up and ready to shoot, I had my Glock out as Parker held on to Val and said, "Well, here we go again, another standoff. I swear this time I will blow her head off."

"Again, you will die, I think my wife will enjoy doing that." I knew Penny was a deadeye shot and she probably could pick him off if Val just gave her a little room. Parker was covering himself well with her body.

"Don't be foolish, I just doubled back passing the idiot cops and came back here to get my car. I had it stashed in the woods by the cabin in case I needed to make a getaway, but didn't count on the cops watching the road.

Doesn't matter, you don't want your friend hurt so back off, I need to get to my car."

"You plan on eventually killing her, it's the way you are, a cold blooded murderer, so you won't let her live. One last kill before you die, right Parker?"

"I don't know, maybe I'll keep this one and make her my slave. She's a looker huh?"

While he was talking, he was moving towards his car slowly. I was moving towards him even slower.

He held up his gun and yelled, "Get back! Don't be a hero. I could kill you but I do respect you as an author. I'm not totally barbaric. Now back off so I don't have to shoot you."

He came around to the passenger side of the station wagon and was going to put Val in, just as we heard another rifle shot and Parker went down.

I was stunned and ran to him, he was still alive and I grabbed his gun from him, pulled my cell phone and dialed Blake. He came on and I said to get back to the cars, I had Parker.

I told Penny to keep her gun on him and went to release Val from her bonds. She stood and grabbed on to me hugging tightly. I looked to the woods across the road and saw something that totally shocked me. I saw someone standing next to a tree, holding a rifle. It was Bonnie Richner. She smiled, gave a little wave to me then went back into the woods and disappeared.

Sunshine State Murders

A few minutes later Blake came busting out of the woods, now totally breathless from running. "Val!" He screamed, and ran to her and grabbed on, holding her tight. They hugged and then Blake looked to me and asked what happened.

"I'll tell you, but you'll never believe it."

All the other officers had regrouped at the cars as Parker was being put in the EMT unit that was called along with the local cops. He was seriously wounded, but would live. I went to the edge of the road looking to see if I could spot Bonnie. She must have been in the car I heard nearby.

Penny came up and asked, "Why did Bonnie do this? What was her motive?"

"Easy, she was a fan and was protecting me."

"Don't go getting a big head now, at least we know she didn't hurt Val. But what about this, her shooting Parker?"

"It was a righteous shoot with a rifle and not a handgun, she saved us and Val, so I'm sure they won't press charges. Although they could say, she was stalking me with the rifle. But I'm not pressing charges." I smiled and kissed Penny on the forehead and we went back to the others.

Blake and Val were sitting on the back of the second EMT unit as the medics were checking Val over. Blake came to us and asked, "You actually saw Bonnie Richner with a rifle and she shot Parker?"

"Yep, my stalker saved the day, that's how I see it."

"Why did she leave? I would have liked to thank her."

"Who knows, maybe she didn't want the attention."

Val called for Blake and he went back to her. Penny heard Willy barking in the van and went to let the dog out. They went to give Willy some relief on the side of the road.

I pulled my cell phone and called Maybell. I didn't know if they radioed him about the incident so I thought I would tell him.

He came on and I said, "I have such a story to tell, are you sitting down?"

*

Chapter 28

We were back in the Palatka police precinct giving our statements to Maybell and his men as they typed and wrote everything out to make it official and have the evidence to prosecute Parker. He was in the hospital under heavy guard and not going anywhere, anytime soon.

Sunshine State Murders

I was sorry that a bookstore owner was actually a serial killer, but it would make a good book someday. I called and filled Morty in on the details and he wanted this story to be published next and asked if I could get on it asap. I said I'd see if I could and we finished.

Val was well enough to avoid having to go back into the hospital, which made her happy. Blake was hovering around her like he was afraid she'd disappear again. They looked so cute together and I had hopes for their relationship. Besides Val had told me she liked a man in uniform.

Penny was sitting in the squad room holding Willy on her lap and watching the circus of activities going around her on to get this case finished up. The discovery of the cabin was an accomplishment and all nine bodies were going to be identified so next of kin could be informed. A welcome relief to many of them.

Maybell was flitting around the precinct getting things organized for a press conference being televised to all major stations around the area from Gainesville to Orlando. A serial killer of this notoriety was something rare, and it turned out that Ken had also killed a number of women in New York according to evidence found in his cabin. Seems he kept souvenirs of all his kills. Something I could never understand about serial killers, was it just something to keep the evidence to snub in the face of the law? Stupid to keep such damning proof.

Penny came over to where I was sitting telling my story to a detective as he filed his report. She pulled up a chair and sat.

"I'm not really looking forward to the rest of the book tour. I just want to go home."

"I'm feeling out of it too. We are getting too old to be working so hard."

"Speak for yourself, old man. I'm just wanting to be back into my own pool and swinging around my stripper pole." When she said that, the detective suddenly was paying attention. Penny smiled and said to him, "I have a stripper pole back home; you can come out anytime to watch me work it."

He gave a nod and went back to his report.

I was holding in a laugh, then Maybell came out and called us to his office. We went down the hall and into the room. Maybell was seated at his desk and was smiling, we sat.

"Ah knew y'all would come out of this good. Ma wife, Flo, said y'all would solve it. Now she's making me miserable with her high faluten attitude. So Bonnie Richner was the one who took down Parker?"

"Well, she was standing in the woods with a rifle just after Parker was took down as you say. I'm not sure why she left and didn't come out to take credit."

"Simple, she had warrants fer her up north for slippin' out of custody in the hospital. Probably figgerd she'd be arrested fer that."

205

"Yes, that's possible, but we may never know, unless they catch her. But I have a feeling she's not wanting to be caught. I wish I could at least thank her. You're not going to charge her with anything?"

"Hell no, she did this city a service, taking down the most heinous serial killer we've had in a good number of years. Forever even."

"Well, maybe someday I'll be able to thank her."

"Write your book about this and dedicate it to her," Maybell said with a laugh.

"That works for me. So are we free to go?"

"Ah wish y'all would git out of town so we kin git back to normal around here."

"Thanks, and it was a pleasure to know you too."

"I'll have a car escort you outta town, so we'll be sure y'all left," Maybell laughed.

"Don't worry we'll will leave as soon as we find out what Val is going to do. Thanks again." Penny and I stood and left the office. We found Val and Blake outside the building after a detective told us where they went.

"Jim, is it all over now?" Val asked.

"Yep, we are no longer needed it seems. But Maybell told me earlier that you would have to testify about the kidnapping and what you saw. So you'd either need to come back or… " I looked to Blake and he smiled.

"Val is stayin' with me for awhile; we have a lot of exploring to do."

"I can work on my edits from Blake's house for Morty, and I'll be around to see the bastard fry."

"Well they have enough on him to have a good barbeque. So Penny and I are climbing into the Flying Book Mobile and heading north to my next book signing."

"The Flying Book Mobile?" Penny said, "I like that, can we have it airbrushed on the side?"

"Hmm, sounds like a plan."

We hugged each other and said our good-byes, Penny and I got into the van and we drove off. I looked into the rearview mirror and saw them watching us go. I'd miss them.

"I called Morty and told him about our adventures and he wants me to write the story into a book, he liked it. He also said the rest of the book tour is still on. But I told him that we would honor the east coast signings, and that was it. We are going back home after Richmond."

"No Washington?" Penny sounded disappointed.

"Well, I think we can go there for a visit since we are up that way, but no work or murders, please."

Sunshine State Murders

~~*~~

The next two weeks were pleasant in the van as we camped along the way. The book signings went well and sold a lot of books making Morty happy.

After we finished the tour, we did go up the coast with the van and stayed a couple days in Washington. I had been there in the sixties when I was in the Army stationed at Fort Belvoir and used to go into D.C. on weekends. So, it was good to see it again. We then went up to New York and stopped in to visit the Traviano family and fill Francis in on how Angelo was doing in his new job as a bodyguard for celebrities. We left there, drove back through to Michigan and stopped for a few days to visit family.

The next week was spent exploring the country and relaxing on the way back home. It was comfortable in the van.

We hit the border of Vegas about a week later and it was a beautiful sight. We drove to the old office and found it empty, I knew this but I wanted to see the sign on the door telling me where they had moved to. I figured they wouldn't tell me, they were a weird bunch.

I consulted my Palm TX to find the address and location of the building and we drove over. It wasn't far from the old office and it was huge. I wondered how expensive this would be, but our cases and Buck's guard business would more that take care of it.

I parked the van and we went into the lobby, it was all glass and well decorated. I looked to the reception counter and saw a girl I didn't know. I figured she was the temp hired by Lacey to help her. We came up to the counter as the girl looked up and smiled.

"Hello, may I help you?"

"No, we just want to visit the place," I said and took Penny to the doors that I presumed went into the inner offices. The girl at the desk was having a fit that we were going in and got on the phone.

We came into an inner waiting room and counter where I saw Lacey sitting on the phone trying calm down the girl out front when she saw it was us. She hung up and screamed, "They're here!!"

I jumped when she did that and looked down the hallway, Buck popped out followed by Trapper. We were all having a good time greeting each other then Earl came out and joined us.

"So how was the tour, did you catch your killer?" Earl asked.

"That's a good story, I'll save it for the barbecue we are going to throw at the house, everyone's invited."

I turned to see the front desk girl come in and Lacey introduced us. I turned to Lacey and said, "You did save me the best office right?"

She flexed her finger into a follow me and led all of us down the hallway. We came to a door that had crime scene yellow tape all over it, with a sign saying "Do not enter under penalty of death!" I laughed and pulled the tape, opening the door. I was startled by a loud ringing and looked up to see the cowbell taped to the back of the door.

Lacey laughed and said, "That's so you don't scare me anymore." Everyone laughed. I was impressed by the office; it was twice as big as my last office. It had wood paneled walls and thick dark blue carpet. There were plenty of shelves and I saw that Lacey had put my books on them. There was a huge oak desk and all my computers were set up. I turned and said, "It's good, thanks."

*

Chapter 29

We were all full from the steaks and fries that we had from our barbecue and were sitting around as I related the story to them. Buck loved the part about the Crossroads Saloon, he had heard of the biker bar from past friends, Trapper was asking about the police set-up in Palatka, once a cop always a cop. Deacon asked if the weather was nice down there, that was Deacon for you.

Penny was very glad to be back and was talking to Lynn, Maria and Earl's girl Paula, in the pool, as the guys sat discussing cases they had while I was out of town. We talked about the new office, it was once a law office for partners who dissolved the partnership and closed up the building. Earl said he got a good rate for it, I remembered how Earl talked the landlord of our second office back in Michigan to give us a good rate.

It was nice to be back, I had missed everyone. I wondered if I would ever do a book tour again. It was fun for a change, the travel was great, got to see a lot of the country. The signings weren't bad, met a lot of nice people and one serial killer.

I excused myself and went into the house. In the kitchen I turned to the window to see all my friends out by the pool and thought back on how this all started. It seemed so long ago. I got another beer from the fridge and opened it, just as my cell phone buzzed. I looked to the caller ID and it said unknown. I answered anyway with a hearty hello.

"Hi Jim, how are you feeling being back home now?"

I paused thinking, then, "Is this Bonnie?"

I could hear her laugh, then she said, "How can you forget your most dedicated fan. I won't bother you, I just called to say I really was glad to meet you and your wife. I'm sorry for that stupid remark to her, I would never have harmed her because I know how important she is to you."

"Bonnie, why did you disappear after the incident in the woods?"

"Jim, they would have returned me to my town to serve time in that nut house, I'm not nuts, just angry at times, so I get a little carried away when people piss me off. The courts didn't understand that I had a lousy childhood and it built up in me. All the frustrations and then someone would look at me wrong and I would get mad. Maybe someday I'll turn myself in for help, but for now I'm living well."

"So how did you end up shooting Parker?"

"After I found out that Steve hit Val but didn't stab her, and I knew I didn't, I started to investigate. I made some calls pretending to be police checking on a case we had, I managed to get some info on Parker. I started to follow him and you around. Did I do good tailing you?"

"Well I have to say I didn't see you."

"Thanks, I followed Parker to Steve's motel the night he died. I saw him go into Steve's room and then come out a while later. He left and I went to look in the window and saw Steve hanging. I knew I had to protect you and Penny. So I followed you around, even down to Orlando, then back up. I saw all the commotion the day Val was taken, I didn't see it happen, but followed you out to Parker's cabin. I hid in the woods and when I saw he had Penny I got my rifle out of my car and waited till I could hit him. I took a shot, but he moved wrong, so I just winged him and then he got away."

"Why do you have a rifle in your car?"

"It was my dad's, he used to take me hunting. He died last year, cancer, and I got the rifle. I carry it with me in case I need to go hunting."

I felt a chill when she said that.

"So how did you end up shooting Parker?" I said again.

"I followed your van up the county road and then into the woods. I parked down the road and went to where you all were parked and waited. Parker made it easy when he got around the passenger side of the car, he opened himself up and I shot. I meant to kill him but just wounded him. I would have taken another shot but he was on the ground and then you came over. I left the woods after you saw me and I'm in the wind as they say." I heard her laugh. "Don't worry Jim I won't bother you again. But please always remember me, I'll always remember you and I'll keep reading your books." She hung up.

I stood with my phone in hand and stared at it. I hoped she meant it when she said she wouldn't bother me again. I felt sorry for her but I didn't need the hassle. Penny came in and saw me looking at my phone.

"What's up Sherlock?"

"I just got a call from Bonnie."

Penny tensed up, I continued, "She says she won't bother us again and she was trying to protect us. I'm going to think she meant that. She said she's in the wind, I hope it's a good wind. I'll fill you in on what all she said later. Shall we go back out to our friends and have a good time?"

She got a few more drinks from the fridge and we went back out. I had to get my mind back to my friends. I sat in my lawn chair and looked around the area, wondering if she was out there watching. Well, I'd worry about that another day.

*

THE END

Preview of the next book, "Blue Suede Murders"

Chapter 1

Elvis hadn't left the building. Why? Because he was dead.

No, not the real Elvis, he died years ago, sitting on the toilet, or so legend or rumor has it. This Elvis wasn't the real Elvis, unless the reports of his death were greatly exaggerated. He once had been seen in Grand Rapids, Michigan working at a burger joint, but that was never proven.

This Elvis in the charred white spangled suit, was barely recognizable, he was burned severely in the pink Cadillac sitting off the Vegas strip by Sahara as the Las Vegas fire department was hosing down the flaming car while the tourists watched nearby. It was a circus for the people as they watched the car finally flame out.

When the scorched metal of the car had cooled, Vegas Metro CSI was on the scene to examine the wreck and the county medical examiner, Joesph Lang, proclaimed the body to be an impersonator. Hardly a surprise.

Lieutenant Lynn Carter, homicide detective and her partner, Sergeant Frank DeAngelo, AKA Deacon, were standing to the side waiting for the okay from the fire department to release the scorched scene. Joe Lang said that the body was possibly doused in some type of flame accelerant and set on fire, so that's why homicide was called in.

"Hey Joe, what can you tell me?" Lynn asked Joe Lang as she was leaning over the charred remains of the classic Cadillac and looking at the body of the victim.

"Well, Elvis has left the world. He was doused in some liquid, probably kerosene from the smell or gasoline and set aflame. The fire spread to the car seats and then engulfed the whole car. The fire on the man's body probably killed him instantly, it usually does. Breathing in the flames and the lungs shut down. Poor bastard, just finished his show at Harrahs and was driving around."

"How do you know that?"

"The valet at Harrahs said he told him, just before he drove out. No one in the area saw the attack, they just saw the fire. Shame, he was so good with his impersonation."

"You know him?"

"Sure, he's the only impersonator with this model of Cadillac. Troy Berlington. Worked the impersonator show at Harrahs, I've seen him a number of times, he was good, very good. Shame he ended this way."

Deacon was listening to all this and said, "He's a hunka, hunka Burning Love now?"

Joe just gave the big man a long uncomfortable stare, shook his head and walked away. Lynn smacked his arm.

"You can be a little insensitive occasionally; didn't you see Joe had a man crush on this guy?"

"I didn't know that Joe was gay."

"Oh Deacon, he's not, he just admired the guy for his talent. Let just get through this okay?"

"Sure, I like Elvis, but I wouldn't have a crush on him."

"Shut up Deacon, let's get to work and figure out who hated Elvis enough to kill him." She went off away from the charred car and to the supervisor of the CSI.

"Paul, as soon as you get some info, let me know."

"Sure Lynn, do you have 'suspicious minds' over this killing, here 'in the ghetto'?"

"Don't you start that too, just get me the info without the song list," She huffed and walked away.

He yelled to her, "Viva Las Vegas!"

Lynn flipped him the bird and kept walking to her car followed by Deacon, trying not to laugh aloud.

~~*~~

The next morning, I rolled out of bed, nearly stepping on our toy Yorkie, Willy. He luckily shot out before my foot hit the floor and I stood. I looked around the bedroom and didn't see my lovely wife and Vegas' favorite talk show host, Penny. I listened for any sound in the house and then heard clanking from the direction of the kitchen. I was worried that Penny was making breakfast, but if it made her happy, I would force myself to eat it.

I went to my personal bathroom; it was nice we each had our own so we could get ready in the morning to go off to our respective jobs without tripping over each other. I was looking in the mirror, studying the new wrinkles showing on my face, thinking about plastic surgery.

Penny and I had just returned from a month long book tour where I signed my novels for adoring fans. Along the way, we met my book editor who was beaten and stabbed in Florida where I was meeting my readers and we ended up catching a serial killer. The best thing about the whole crime was Val, my book editor, met a nice young cop and I bought the motorhome van of my dreams.

We drove across country in the van and I now had it parked in the drive. Since it was as small as a normal van, I could drive it around and let my classic '89 Crown Vic rest in the garage. The interior of the van was as roomy as a motorhome, complete with kitchen, bathroom and bedroom. I figured that I could drive it around town and also use it as a mobile office and home away from home.

I finished up in the bathroom and headed to the kitchen ready for the worst. I turned the corner and saw Penny sitting at the snack bar watching our friend and former mob enforcer, Angelo making breakfast. I had forgotten that he was staying in our guesthouse and he loved to slip in to make us one of his famous breakfasts. I didn't object, they were very good and he enjoyed it, besides it would mean Penny wouldn't be cooking.

"Good morning everyone," I said as I came up to my wife and gave her a sloppy kiss.

"You're in a good mood this morning," she said wiping her mouth with a napkin.

I suddenly realized that she had maple syrup on her lips and I now tasted it on mine. It was good.

"I'm happy to be back home and going to my new office to set it up," I said.

Angelo came over and said, "Morning Mr. R., you sleep well?"

"I did Angelo, and thank you for watching the house while we were away."

"My pleasure, I didn't even use the pool," he said like it was an accomplishment.

"Angelo, we told you that you could use the pool if you wanted to," Penny spoke.

"I was afraid I might drown, and there'd be no one to save me."

"You could have invited someone to swim with you," I said before I realized that Angelo didn't know anyone out here. "Angelo, we have to get you some friends."

"Most the people I know are all in prison or on

the run. I could join some social club but I don't think you want a bunch of wiseguys from the mob hanging around your house. We'll think of something."

I flipped on the TV to see what the forecast for weather in the Vegas valley had in store for us. There was a news reporter from Penny's station, KLAS, talking about an early morning car fire on the strip. He went on to explain that an Elvis impersonator was found in the burned out car. As the camera was scanning the scene, I caught a glimpse of Lynn and Deacon standing by the car. Penny made a little squeal of delight seeing them and laughed. Then Penny said, "Someone torched Elvis, oh that is so tragic."

I wasn't sure if she was kidding or serious.

Nearly two years ago, my beautiful wife and I flew into Vegas from Michigan to get married. We got involved in the Bridezilla murders and were almost married by an Elvis minister, much to Penny's dismay.

She definitely wasn't a big fan of Elvis, she never admitted it to her viewing public, she knew Elvis was revered here and didn't want hate mail. But when she found out that Elvis was to preside over our wedding she went ballistic. Luckily, Lynn had connections with a local minister from a mission in the downtown area who came in to save the ceremony. We were married on that day and were living happily ever after, so far.

Penny realized that she was supposed to be on the road to her station, so jumped up and went off to finish getting ready. I had my breakfast and thanked Angelo for it. Penny had breezed out the door saying good-bye to us and was gone. I worried that she would kill herself rushing one day.

I finished getting ready and told Angelo I was leaving. He said he had to go out and protect some recording executive today and would see us later.

I got in the van and drove out to the new building where we had moved our investigating business. It was a really nice brick and chrome building and huge. Which was good for us, now having three P.I.'s and all of Buck's one hundred and ten security guards, our last building was a bit crowded. I had only been in the building once since I got back from my tour, so I hadn't had time to set my office up. This was going to be my day to get settled in.

I drove in and parked. Going through the front door, I met with the new receptionist that Lacey hired and she remembered me from the other day when Penny and I returned to storm into the building. I walked through the second set of doors and didn't see Lacey at her desk. I walked down the hallway and into my office, I stood looking around when all of a sudden something dropped down hanging from the ceiling. It was a skeleton on a noose rope!

Lacey and Buck came into the room laughing. Buck said, "Looks like murder is following you from the old office."

*

Continued in the book...

Jim Richards Family of Readers

Thanks to the following people who are now part of the Jim Richards Family of Readers. They have read a book or more and enjoyed them. They all volunteered to be included in the list. If you are a fan of the books, send me your full name and you will be included in future books. Send your name to murdernovels@bobmoats.com to be added here and on the website.

* Achim Feifel * Al Norris * Alex Wheatley * Alexandra Delporte-Wilkinson * Amy Tapia * Andrea Bryan * Anne Shepherd * Arianda Sugar * Arlene Markowski * Ashley Augustus * Audra Hall * Barbara Hughes * Barbara Sammons * Barbara Schuler * Barbara Zirger * Beth Donohue Plenskofski * Betsy Childress * Beth Gibson * Bill Sandy * Bill Tornquist * Billie-jo Collie * Boni J Rychener * Carl Bishopric * Carla Lewis * Carole Henderson * Carolyn Conroy * Carolyn Riddle-Linington

Bob Moats

* Cassy Bailey * Chad Hudson * Charlotte L Duran * Cheryl L. Everett * Cindy Ackley Nunn * Cindy Valstad * Connie Bancroft * Corinne Kay O'Daniel * Dana Robbins Chuchran * Dana Wichita * Danielle Monique * Darren Heald * Dave Travers * David Wilkinson * DeAnn Jannereth * Deanna Miller * Deb Breuker Balbo * Debbie Carter * Debbie White * Deborah Fartuch * Deborah Gauze * Deborah Sullivan * Dee King * Denise Freeman * Diana Carver * Dixie Beck * Donna Gould * Donna Thompson * Donny Minter * Doris Kight * Eddie Moore * Eric Walters * Felicia Annette Bradfield * Francine Menor * Gail Chesney * Georgiann Minster * George Conner * Greg Colucci * Hayley Rankin * Harold Garcia * Heidi Arnold * Irma Ranee Coy * Jacqueline Moss * Jan Kimball * Janice Schneider * Janice Spoor * Jennifer Redmond * Jessica Keown-Belous * Jim Beck * Jo Boguslaw * Jo Turner * Joanne Marie Turner * John Peiffer * John Wisbiski * Joseph Wauro * Joyce Stacy * Joyce Trifiletti * Judy Franklin * Judy Travers * Judy Padgett * Julie Heath * Junnahvee Benson * Karen Dahl * Karen Grams * Karen Higham * Karen Kaiser * Karen Meinburg Richwine * Karen Kirkman Parker * Karin Hawkins * Karin Vasvari * Kathleen Donohue Roesing * Kathleen Riddle-Wolfe * Kathy Hinds Moore * Kathy Jones * Kathy Mitchell * Katie Benzler * Kay Burns * Kelly Garcia * Ken Boggs * Keota Rodriguez * Kiera Mccarthy * Kim Estes * Kitty Stolle * Kristie Sciler * Kirsty Stanton * LaLonnie Scallen * Larry Morris * Leann Parr * Lenora Scales * Leslie Marie Jackson * Linda Forester * Linda Ingle Cox * Linda Kennerö * Linda Magill * Lisa Bower * Liz Gibson * Lorraine Wiman * Loretta Alexander * Lynda Bowles * Lynette Lawrance * LuAnn Louttit * Manny Rothman * Marcia Gibson DeWitt * Marie Calder * Marlene Bryan * MaryLouise Kramp * Mary Lynn Gross * Megan Atkins *

223

Sunshine State Murders

Meghan Hyden * Melody Cannavan * Michael Carruthers * Michael Dinkens * Michael Vannoy * Michelle Burns-Mitchell * Michelle Pilcher * Micki Potter * Mike Moats * Mimi Baur * Myrna Hecht * Nadine Sutton * Natalie Quine * Neena Martin * O'Della Wilson * Pat Pollington * Pat Rohn * Patricia Jarmon * Patricia C Trezza * Patrick Barry * Paul Lawrance * Peggy Davis * Phyllis Bassett * Raylene Matheny * Rebecca Collins Besner * Renee Brumley * Reta Hanna * Reta Moats * Roberta Navarro-Harder * Sally Berneathy * Sally Hubler * Sarah Santos * Satka Nikc * Sharon E. Edwards * Sharon Mangini * Sharon McMillon * Sheena Rawl * Sherry Amstutz * Shirley Alvarez * Shirley Davies * Shirley Williams * Stacie Rowe * Stephanie Conner * Steve Cullen * Susan Haughton * Susan Hesse Adams * Susan Salomon * Suzan K Chase * Taisha Cullum * Tamara Moore * Tammy Castleberry * Tammy Lynn Wood * Ted Murphy * Terri Atkins * Terri Creech * Terry Raab * Tonia Rachael Riggs-Williams * Travis Fleury-Lopez * Twyla Gawlas * Val Brooks * Walt Munsel * Yvonne Isakson *

Thank you to all these wonderful people.

Thank you for purchasing this book. I hope you enjoy it as much as I enjoyed writing it for my faithful readers. Please feel free to email me to tell me what you thought about my stories. I love hearing from the readers. I can be reached at murdernovels@bobmoats.com thanks again!

www.ingramcontent.com/pod-product-compliance
Lightning Source LLC
Chambersburg PA
CBHW070814120626
46556CB00002B/497